# *Are You Enjoying?*

# Are You Enjoying?

## · Stories ·

## MIRA SETHI

ALFRED A. KNOPF  New York

2021

THIS IS A BORZOI BOOK
PUBLISHED BY ALFRED A. KNOPF

www.aaknopf.com

Knopf, Borzoi Books, and the colophon are registered trademarks
of Penguin Random House LLC.

Library of Congress Cataloging-in-Publication Data
Names: Sethi, Mira, [date] author.
Title: Are you enjoying? / Mira Sethi.
Description: First edition. | New York : Alfred A. Knopf, [2021] |
"This is a Borzoi Book"
Identifiers: LCCN 2020039135 (print) | LCCN 2020039136 (ebook) |
ISBN 9781524732875 (hardcover) | ISBN 9781524732882 (ebook)
Subjects: LCGFT: Short stories.
Classification: LCC PR9540.9.S466 A88 2021 (print) |
LCC PR9540.9.S466 (ebook) | DDC 823/.92—dc23
LC record available at https://lccn.loc.gov/2020039135
LC ebook record available at https://lccn.loc.gov/2020039136

Jacket hand illustration based on a photograph by billyfoto / Getty Images

Jacket design by Janet Hansen

Manufactured in the United States of America
First Edition

*For Ami and Abu*

She had a new feeling, the feeling of danger; on which a new remedy rose to meet it, the idea of an inner self or, in other words, of concealment.

—HENRY JAMES, *What Maisie Knew*

*Zara Sa Jhoom Loun Mein*
*Arey Na Re Na Re Na*
*Zara Sa Ghoum Loun Mein*
*Arey Na Re Na Re Na*

*[Shall I Dance a Little?*
*Oh No No No*
*Shall I Sway a Little?*
*Oh No No No]*
—Lyrics from the movie
*Dilwale Dhulania Le Jayenge*

# Contents

Mini Apple

*3*

Breezy Blessings

*31*

A Life of Its Own—Part One

*51*

A Man for His Time

77

Tomboy

99

A Life of Its Own—Part Two

*123*

Are You Enjoying?

*141*

*Are You Enjoying?*

# Mini Apple

Around 11:00 a.m., slack-limbed and sighing on the toilet seat, eyes closed, Javed heard a rap on the bathroom door. He opened his eyes to the broken first flood of daylight. It was typical of the cook, these days Javed's only house help, to disturb his delicate morning routine.

"Ye-es?" Javed said, his voice neutral, as if speaking across a glass door in an office.

"A *gori* madam is at the front door," the cook mumbled.

As his fingers unclenched from the Muslim shower he was holding, Javed gulped back his sleeping breath. He'd gone to bed at 5:00 a.m., after recording a special report on the state of Pakistani democracy in his studio at Jeet TV.

"Show her to the drawing room. Use your common sense. And don't disturb me in the potty next time."

Javed had become even more of a workhorse six months before, after a raw and, he thought, unnecessary divorce.

He peeled the nightshirt off his chest and let it fall to the floor. He looked in the mirror and breathed deliberately: once, and twice, three times, four times. These days a little meditation went a long bloody way. He brushed his teeth and walked back to his swampy bedroom. The bedsheets were soft with humidity. Javed threw on a clean *kameez* over his *shalwar* and sprayed Issey Miyake on his neck.

As he walked into the drawing room, Javed smiled to buoy his own confidence. "Aha! How *nice* to see you." The good thing about being a television personality was that even in his gloomiest moments he could transform his mood at a moment's notice. Tone of voice, steadiness of gaze, the spring in his smile: these aspects of himself now operated without effort, with the cold autonomy of need. Marianne Almond, an economic officer at the American embassy, had set foot in his house for the first time, but he knew her. He knew she lived in a house across his street; he'd seen her jogging in the neighborhood several times, a police officer always sprinting behind her.

"Sorry to have barged in," said Marianne, a pale hand raised, as if testing for rain. "I figured you'd be home today." She was wearing brown linen trousers and a black T-shirt. She had clear green eyes, and Javed saw that she was almost as tall as he was. Her eyebrows were so sparse light bounced off them.

She sat down on his plastic-covered sofa.

"Do you have time to chat?" she asked.

"Absolutely," Javed smiled, sitting on the sofa in front of her. "There's an insect on your knee—"

"I'm having a party at my house tomorrow—

"Go on," she said. She swept a hand into her hair with the studied patience of a foreign dignitary. Then she cupped the beetle in her palm, set it on the floor.

"Would you like something to drink?" asked Javed.

"Oh, it appears your drinking pipes are leaking. My staff noticed the leak. You might want to get that checked."

"I have bottled water. I'll bring you a fresh bottle."

To his relief he found two small bottles of Nestlé in the fridge. He grabbed a clean glass from the cabinet and brought the items to Marianne on a tray. He removed the cap in front of her.

"That's very kind of you," she said. She took a sip from the bottle and placed it between her feet.

*That's very kind of you.* People in Pakistan had stopped uttering statements such as *that's very kind of you*. No one said *that's very kind of you* when you brought them water. The utterance reminded Javed of the photos he'd seen of Marianne at the launches of restaurants, boutiques, movie premieres, and inaugurations. In each photo, she had a that's-very-kind-of-you air about her: eyes beaming with apology, face bashful with delight. That people invited her to cultivate proximity was obvious enough: Marianne Almond could always help in the facilitation of a visa. But they also jostled around her to inhale the source of her pristine foreignness, her teasing jokes, her voluminous brown hair that shone brassy in the Islamabad sun.

"Anyway," said Marianne, interrupting Javed's reverie. "I'm having a party at my place tomorrow. The guests will be a smattering of journos and diplomats. Join us if you can. I've been an appalling neighbor. Goodness. I've been meaning to extend an invitation for a *long* time." And she rolled her eyes at her own unearthed delinquency.

"Don't be silly," said Javed. "It's so nice that you came here. I will certainly try. I have a prior engagement," he fibbed. "But it's not so important. If I get done early I'll be there with bells on."

"Wonderful. I look forward to seeing you then," said Marianne. She got up and smoothed the pleats of her trousers.

Javed couldn't think of anything more to say, and she was already on her feet and waving goodbye with a twirl of her long fingers.

From the moment Marianne Almond had arrived in Islamabad two years before, during which time Javed had gotten married *and* divorced—his infant daughter lived with his ex-wife—he'd been reassured by an American presence across the road. Marianne had broken with tradition and chosen to live outside the Diplomatic Enclave—the sprawling complex of houses, gyms, grocery stores, tennis courts—where most ambassadors and embassy officers resided. Her decision was sanctioned by the Embassy, if unusual. The security architecture installed by her team had upgraded Javed's neighborhood. Once a dusty expanse of eucalyptus-shaded bungalows, Green Acres now looked like the suburb of a spotless city: steel barriers, spikes, ramps, and towers padded by sandbags dotted most streets. The black-and-yellow concrete barriers had turned the roads into go-kart courses. "No security issues," Javed would say to his friends. "Amreecans live here. Security is outstanding."

Javed had switched to political commentary after fifteen full years as a television actor. He'd been a graceful presence on the screen, his gaze touched with roguish charm. When his first movie came out, in the early nineties, he'd had a business card emblazoned with the words *Film Star.* His friends had sniggered, and he'd burned all two hundred cards. A few years later Pakistan's national channel had approached Javed to consider hosting his own talk show: he was selling himself short by being just an actor. He had more to offer the world, the producer said, like his wit and charisma. Javed had turned down the proposition. He had been, at the time, unsure of his ability to discuss, cleverly, culture and politics for a whole hour. Television had a way of revealing the inner truth of the host.

By the time privately funded channels came around, in the 2000s, Javed was in his late thirties, at the peak of his acting career. Umeed TV lured him with a package he couldn't refuse: coanchoring a news show with his then-girlfriend of three years. They were a power couple, beloved, on the verge of marriage. His girlfriend, a lawyer, had said the opportunity was the culmination of everything she had dreamed of. Javed's analyses—critiquing the corruption of the ruling party, India's belligerence, American interference in global affairs—had been widely praised on TV. What most people didn't know was that Javed typed out his bare thoughts into bullet points; his girlfriend spun them into stunning discourses.

After a year of sitting next to each other four days a week behind a long red desk—of Javed occasionally pinching his girlfriend's thigh behind it—she'd told him she was having an affair with the owner of the channel. Her expression was one of flat, unerring conviction, the same look she emitted to her viewers during a broadcast. She didn't know where the relationship with the boss would go, she said, but she was certain she wanted to pursue it.

It was around this time that Javed, stricken, presented himself as a sacrificial offering. His parents reminded him he was approaching forty, that he was mad to still be single, so he said yes to his mother and his father. Actually what he said was yes—yes—yes, find me someone and I shall marry her. Then came Sameena, a marriage, a child, a rapid divorce.

After Marianne left, Javed fidgeted with his wristwatch and looked around. The torpor within him had been dislodged. Now that he was awake, he wondered what he would do for the rest of the afternoon. He said, "Allah ho Akbar," with a long exhaling sigh to relieve a peculiar mounting restlessness. Though Javed lived alone, he'd observed that silences unsettled him: they rang in his skull, set his nerves on edge.

He walked around his house with curiosity, poking his head into dirty corners—behind the fridge, over the soot-stained wall above the oven—in astonishment at how seamlessly the order in his home had collapsed in the absence of his ex-wife. He didn't miss Sameena, but his home had looked and smelled pleasant while she'd been around. These days going back to sleep often seemed like a sensible choice—if only he could truly *sleep*. He touched the blackened wall above the oven and looked at his smeared finger. Why had Marianne come bearing the invitation for the party? She could have sent a card; she could have asked any of her friends in the media for Javed's phone number.

He meandered back to the drawing room to see it anew through her eyes. The walls were covered with framed photos of his parents and siblings and daughter. The room wasn't sumptuous, but it was a picture of restrained dignity: a large red carpet bathed in afternoon light, sofas covered in plastic like expensive new cars.

He wondered if he should go to the party the next day.

He knew from experience that a little withholding went a long way.

For now, he would drive to the home of his former in-laws to see his daughter, Inaya. Before the divorce Sameena had complained that Javed's working hours left him no time for their small family. She'd texted him verses from Rumi, urging him to realize the wound was where the light entered.

He hadn't responded. Not once.

One day, she'd returned to her wealthy parents.

As Javed held his daughter in Sameena's home, he was relieved to see Inaya gurgling with laughter at the slightest provocation: when Javed widened his eyes, when he touched and withdrew his hand from Inaya's leg in repetitive fashion. His own face was thwacked with tiny hands, his chin streaked with spit. Sameena didn't so much as offer him a cup of tea.

The next day, as a sound technician pinned a microphone inside Javed's shirt, he thought of the way Marianne's smile had lingered as she'd said *I figured you'd be home today*.

He resolved to skip her party.

On his way back from work he stopped at the supermarket and bought three crates of Nestlé bottled water. He bought bags of ice. He called up a friend to procure the number of a bootlegger, and ordered from Vicky Boot—the name under which his friend had saved the contact—bottles of red wine, scotch, and vodka. On the phone Vicky Boot spoke in a guarded tone; the indolence in his voice annoyed Javed until he realized that Vicky's lagging manner was its own learnt protection.

Marianne's party came and went. When Javed didn't hear from her the day after, he curled under a cotton sheet and watched his most-viewed clips on YouTube.

·

Three days later, around 10:00 p.m., Javed heard the doorbell ring. He'd just gotten home from work, and his heart sped up as he switched on the air conditioner in his bedroom. He took off his white dress shirt and put on a white linen shirt. He spat in the sink and rushed to the door.

A police officer was standing next to Marianne. He was tall and square-jawed; a black handgun jutted from the holster around his waist.

"Any problem? Everything okay?" asked Javed.

"Jaav-ed!" said Marianne. "He's here for my security. Nothing to worry about. May I come in?"

"Of course."

Javed invited the officer in but he said he'd prefer to stay outside.

Javed led Marianne to the drawing room. "One moment, please."

He returned with a bottle of scotch, a juice jar full of water, a bottle of wine, and a bucket of ice. Some spicy peanuts in a bowl.

"What would you like to drink? What may I pour you?"

"You're all so frantically—adorably—hospitable."

"It's in our genes."

"But just a tiny bit." She raised her index finger. "Red, please. Won't you have any?"

"I don't drink. Sadly." And he shrugged.

"Why not?"

"Don't like the taste. Honestly."

"How come I didn't see you at my party?"

"I was with my daughter," said Javed, fibbing, since he'd seen Inaya the day before the party. "She lives with her mother and I get to see her once a week."

"Ah, right," said Marianne. "The American ambassador asked

after you. She was complimenting your show on the recent case of land grabbing in Karachi." She took a sip of wine from the glass, looking at Javed over the rim. "'Brave of him to do it,' she said."

"The channel wasn't happy. They say I 'cost' them too much." He took a deep breath. "But that's jolly nice of the ambassador," he said, and felt the intrusion of "jolly"—a word unpracticed on his tongue—hang awkwardly in the air.

He said, "The three of us should do dinner soon. *InshaAllah*."

"That would be great. It seems you're busier than ever."

"Not really."

"Oh good."

Then swiftly, but smoothly, Javed reached for the tips of Marianne's fingers and kissed her hand. It was an old trick, the gesture courteous, restrained, poised on the edge of chivalry—or possibly something more. When Javed lifted his eyes to observe Marianne's face, she was staring back at him, dumbly stunned, as if what he had done was strange yet somehow acceptable. Her lips were neither open nor sealed, but set in an uncertain moue. It was as if she was about to whisper, *That was very kind of you.*

She cleared her throat. "How do you think the government is doing these days?"

"Completely clueless."

"It's a nightmare, isn't it."

"Everyone in the world should have a right to vote in the U.S. election, however," said Javed.

"That's interesting." She was smiling. "But what a relief. For us, I mean. Anyway, I should get going," she said and put her glass down. With her fingers she raked her hair into a crinkled bun. "I hope you managed to get those pipes fixed."

"Not yet. The leak isn't so bad. Let me show you out."

After she'd gone, Javed stared at himself in the mirror for a long time. He saw a divorced workaholic who could, if he really wanted, seize happiness at this late, wrecked stage in his life.

Marianne did not return the next day, or the day after. Javed had recorded a two-day segment on the energy crisis in Pakistan. He'd said solar-driven energy was the way forward, that the American government was going out of its way to provide Pakistan with sustainable solutions. It didn't help to be pro-American these days, but he'd slipped in a compliment, and he wondered if she'd seen the show.

He rushed home as soon as he finished recording in his studio. He lay on his bed, slightly red in the face when he didn't hear from Marianne. The ceiling fan whirred. He told himself not to worry. He would have to be patient.

Or he would have to be proactive.

He picked up his phone. He told his research assistant to comb Google for the words "Marianne Almond." He wanted *all* the information, especially the stuff that seemed irrelevant.

The next morning his assistant dropped off a file at Javed's house. Javed spent the morning huddled in his bedroom, orange highlighter in hand, going through a stack of printouts. He smiled as he highlighted the word "divorce" in a Saturday profile of Marianne. He noted her decision to retain her ex-husband's last name—it was easy to pronounce in the parts of the world in which she worked, she'd said: Almond, just like the nut.

Around noon Javed showered, changed into blue jeans and a lilac polo, and walked across to Marianne's house.

"I'd like to see Marianne," he told the officer outside her gate.

"All right," said the officer. "You have an appointment?"

"Just tell her Javed is here. From that house." He pointed to his wrought-iron gate.

"Like I asked, sir, do you have an appointment?"

"It's Saturday!"

"I'm sorry, you can't go in without preapproval."

"If you tell her my name, she'll be okay with it."

"Let me see what I can do." As the officer crackled his walkie-talkie, Javed heard a familiar voice: "Jaav-ed!"

He turned around.

How pretty she looked.

"It's okay." She waved to the officer. "Let him through." She was standing by the main door in jeans and a loose faded T-shirt printed with the words *Yes We Can*. Her feet were bare and her T-shirt dug a sharp V into the surf of her breasts. Three bars of sunlight pooled over her face, and seeing her framed in the doorway in her shoeless feet, her décolletage shimmering in the sun, Javed felt a tingle of delight at the sudden hidden provocation of the afternoon.

He was led through a hallway, patted down, his shoes, wallet, and keys put through an X-ray scanner, then handed back to him by a younger-looking security official.

Marianne laid a hand on the officer's shoulder. "Thanks, Imran."

She pointed to an open door. "I'll be with you in a second, Jaav-ed."

He walked into a vast, gray-carpeted, bureaucratic-smelling room. Plaques of Plexiglas lined the main shelf to the side of her desk: an award from the Pakistan Greens recognizing Marianne Almond as an environmental leader, another from the Government of Pakistan lauding her efforts to push renewable energy in the Punjab province, and one from the State Department honoring her commitment to public service. Behind her desk, a framed map of Minnesota—a cartoonish profile of a man with a long beak—hung next to a framed map of the Punjab.

Marianne walked into the room, a soccer ball in her hand.

"Made in Sialkot." She smiled.

She breezed past him like a headmistress inspecting the lineup for morning assembly.

"How are you, by the way?" she asked.

"Very well, thanks." He paused. "All the better for seeing you." He motioned with his hands that she should throw the ball to him, and she lobbed it.

"The soccer World Cup balls are all made here," said Javed. "I mean in Pakistan."

"I'm not a bad player myself," she smiled.

"Are you not!"

"What would you like to drink? Lemonade?"

"That would be lovely."

Marianne placed the order on the intercom in Urdu—*"Dou nimbu paani shukria"*—the words stacked together as if *shukria* were part of the drink. Her identity fragmented for a moment into that of a child in a foreign land.

She took three scarves from the top drawer of her desk and laid them out. "This one"—she trailed a finger over an orange scarf—"is from Larkana." She looked up. "And this is from one of the Afghan shops in Jinnah Super. And this, oh, my *favorite,* a woman at Faisal *masjid* just *gave it to me.* I said no but she insisted I have it. Isn't it beautiful?"

The words—Larkana, Sialkot, *masjid* in lieu of "mosque"—slipped from her mouth like air. Her pronunciation was far from perfect, but what a thing her confidence was!

"Frankly, I'm quite amazed by you," said Javed. "By your resourcefulness, your positivity, your decision to live here. God knows this country is neither safe nor easy. I'm amazed by your courage—worn so lightly. It's a hard place in which to plant roots."

Marianne looked at him. She was quiet. She met his gaze. "I appreciate that."

She knotted the orange scarf around her neck. "I wanted to live outside the enclave to experience the real Pakistan. It's important to me. It's important to immerse oneself."

Javed strode across the carpet and kissed her on her hair. He'd meant to kiss her lips, but her height unsettled him, and the gesture spilled into solemnity. The blinds in the room were drawn. At first, Marianne didn't respond. She stood stiffly erect, as if up against a wall. Then, she placed a palm on his cheek, and brushed her lips against his.

Javed could hear his heart thrashing inside his ears.

She led him to the sofa, where she shifted her buttocks deeper into the creased leather upholstery. She touched Javed's nose. "You're sweet."

He blushed and looked at the carpet. "You don't watch my current affairs show?"

"My Urdu isn't *that* great."

He laughed.

"I'm sure it's brilliant," she said. "But, listen. This"—she pointed a finger at Javed, at herself—"is tricky."

"I understand. Of course."

"You're not in the government, so it's technically *fine,* but we have to be careful about this kind of thing. Only for security purposes. As I'm sure you understand."

"You shouldn't have to worry about anything. I've lived across from you for two years."

"This reporter at my party—when I brought you up she said she was engaged to you at some point. She didn't say more."

"She left me. For the owner of the channel where she and I used to work."

Marianne's eyes softened. "Sorry, Jaav-ed."

"Soon after she ditched me I got married very quickly. That too was a disaster." And he laughed wearily.

"Oh dear."

"She wanted to make it work but I was too busy getting my show going."

"Sorry to hear that."

"You don't have to be sorry."

Marianne fidgeted with her opal drop earring. She had beautiful fingers, long and clean, like a librarian's. Then briskly she got up from the sofa, her arms crossed over her chest.

Javed didn't want to sink the mood. "I'll check in with you soon," he said, standing up. He kissed her shoulder and walked out the door, past the security scanner, past her guard—whose stare he ignored—and onto the barricaded road, where he breathed a sigh of complicated relief.

When the map on the wall confirmed what he'd read of Marianne, that she was from Minneapolis, Javed set about reading everything he could about the city. He memorized the names of its historic sites of protest, its most famous parks—Minnehaha

Park, Chain of Lakes, St. Anthony Falls—the names of re-
nowned politicians who'd come from the city. The next time he
saw her it was at his home, two days later.

The formality of their last encounter had disappeared. She
rang a triple chime *ding-ding-ding,* and as soon as Javed opened
the door she leaned in to hug him. He noticed that she'd ditched
her security guard.

Javed handed Marianne a glass of wine as he sat beside her on
the red damask sofa in his living room.

The TV screen was split into three: a male anchor with coal-
black hair to the left, Maulana Amin of the Islamic Board in the
middle, a female anchor to his right. The Maulana was asked
his opinion on the recent talk on social media of reviving Basant,
a kite-flying festival that had been banned by the government
several years before. The government had argued that the string
attached to kites was coated with glass: as the kites fell from the
sky they often landed on the necks of cyclists and motorcyclists,
leading to instant death. Dozens died every year. And since the
illegal manufacturing of glass-coated string could not be halted,
Basant would remain banned.

Maulana Amin rubbed his eyes, his stomach a gushing sack
in the center of the screen. "Basant is a Hindu festival," he said.
"It was never part of Pakistani culture. That is why it should
stay banned." He raised a finger. "Today I hereby issue a *fatwa*
against all those Pakistanis who are promoting this Hindu
festival—"

"Sir," the lady interrupted. "Public opinion shows that most
Pakistanis miss flying kites."

"I will give a *fatwa*." He hiccuped. His speech was slurred.

The anchors cast their gaze downward. A moment later they

cut him off. "Oh, Maulana *sahab*!" said Marianne. "He came to the Ambassador's house recently and guzzled half a bottle of Black Label."

"Openly?"

"Of course. With us they're open."

"God, the hypocrisy. He wants to prove his moderate credentials to you," said Javed.

"There are, like, fifty liberals in this country and I've met *all* of them." Her mouth was slack, in exaggerated disdain, like that of a comedian. "The 'silent majority' isn't interested in secularism or liberalism *or* for that matter fundamentalism." She took a big gulp of the wine. "Folks just want economic uplift."

Javed took a sip of his soda. He was listening.

"The conservative elites are definitely my favorite," she chuckled. "At least they're consistent: no sleeveless, no *sharaab*!" She tapped her finger against her wineglass. "And what about you?"

"What about me?"

"Leftist? Bhuttoist? Closet Islamist?"

"That's right: you don't watch my show. How would you know?"

She flared her nostrils.

She grazed her lips against his.

He led her to the bedroom, where she drank, slowly, another glass of wine. With her toes she peeled off the back straps of her sandals and climbed into his bed, cool in the vacancy of the afternoon. Their clothes were off before Javed could get nervous. He was astonished at the ease of the process, at Marianne's instinctiveness guiding his own. He was accustomed to more tortured maneuverings, conversations held in codes of innuendo. He buried his face in her chest, scented like cake. He tipped her left breast upward with his fingers. "Mini apple," he said. "Mini apple being the nickname of Minneapolis."

Her face collapsed into laughter. Javed saw crow's-feet, elegant in their translucence, in the corners of her eyes.

"You're supersweet," she was saying.

Afterward, she asked him about his daughter. He said Inaya was just under a year old, that she was a piece of his heart. His ex-wife, when they were still married, had wanted him to leave his job on TV, he told Marianne. He'd declined to do so, and, soon after, she'd left him, saying his career in the media had ruined him, that he acted like he was still a bachelor. He hadn't at all, he said. He missed his daughter dearly.

Javed laid his head on Marianne's chest, feeling the rise and ebb of her breath.

"Why didn't you have children," he asked.

"I never wanted kids."

"And your ex-husband?"

"He was happy to go along with what I wanted. He's all right. We talk sometimes." Her green eyes flickered. "He worries about me."

"Why does he worry?"

"Because I'm in Pakistan, of course."

Javed sat up. He held her shoulders. "You shouldn't worry. Pakistan has embraced you. And you fit in so well."

She brushed her thumb against Javed's eyes. "It's nice here with you." She looked down at her bare breasts. "Mini apples, eh?"

"Would you prefer another, more obvious, fruit?"

She laughed. "I *like* mini apple. How clever of you. It can be our little secret."

.

Javed and Marianne saw each other twice a week—in the after-
noons or at night, depending on their schedules—once at his
house, once at hers. They made love right away, and talked
afterward. Javed longed to know the names of the journalists
and lawyers and politicians with whom she frequently dined.
Once he knew he could decide whether or not to feel anxious.
It was too early in their relationship, if he could call it that, to
ask her. Marianne shared select details of her social life in Islamabad, and Javed was smart enough not to prod.

One evening, as Marianne was standing in the kitchen of her
home making an avocado sandwich, Javed asked her what Minneapolis was like. She said quickly and flatly that she disliked
it. She was wearing billowy white pajamas and a white tank top.
Her hair had been hurried, without a pin or a clasp, into a bun.

Her parents had not gotten along, Marianne told him, and
going back to Minneapolis filled her with a nagging sadness.
That was one of the reasons why, she said, she'd taken a job that
enabled her to see the world. She couldn't stay in one place for
too long; she became restless. Pakistan was not without its share
of troubles, she said, but it was "resilient as hell." Javed told her
she seemed comfortable in Islamabad and she agreed.

"By the way," he said. "When you came over to invite me for
the party: Was that a pretext?"

She raised an eyebrow. "For?"

"This. Us."

A ringing laugh, at once wild and surrendering, and a toss of
her head that sent her hair cascading onto her breasts.


Another weekend rolled along, and Javed canceled his social
engagements. Instead, he went shopping for snacks. He bought

artisanal cheeses, hummus, crackers, lime cordial, soda water, tonic. He bought hand towels and arranged them in his bathroom. He sponged the sooty wall behind the kitchen stove. With a thistle broom he swept behind the oven, scraping out burnt matchsticks, Cheerios meshed with human hair, a cracked tennis ball. He scraped out a couple of dead roaches from under the sink cabinet, flicked them to a corner.

When the cook said he felt embarrassed watching Javed clean, Javed looked him dead in the eye. "The only thing permanent in life is change," he divulged.

He gave the cook two weeks off.

Javed arranged a list of songs on his phone—Nusrat Fateh Ali Khan, the Beatles, Abida Parveen—waiting for the moment when Marianne would ring the bell, and he'd rush to the door, the silence between them a promise of things to come. He chilled bottles of beer and wine, bought air fresheners and new underwear. He felt comfortable walking around in front of Marianne in his underwear, a hand patting the flatness of his stomach, as if the action ensured slimness. Marianne laughed at him, told him he was image-obsessed. "The camera puts on fifteen pounds," he told her, grudging the fact as much as he was transfixed by it.

Marianne liked red wine, and Javed made sure he had a new bottle for her every week, though she never drank more than two glasses. He admired her discipline, and tasting the sour wine on her mouth made him stiff with desire.

She asked him, while they were sitting on his bed, what the real reason was for his abstinence. He told her his father had liked his drink a bit too much.

"We have more in common than you realize," she said, stretching her legs. "My mother was an alcoholic. I went through a period in college when I didn't drink. Then I realized how stupid that was: a reaction. You should try it sometime."

He said he would, if they traveled abroad together.

On an overcast April afternoon, as Javed and Marianne sat on a glazed wicker settee in her veranda looking out at the garden, Marianne asked Javed if he wanted to go for a drive in her SUV.

A light rain had begun to fall, and the raindrops trickling into the two-tiered stone fountain in the garden created a feeling of nostalgia, as if it were a scene from one of Javed's old films. It occurred to him it had been nearly three weeks since he'd seen Inaya. He longed to introduce his kid to Marianne, perhaps take them to a restaurant. He could imagine a life in which Marianne encouraged him to be a better father. He could imagine accomplishing quite a lot with her at his side.

"I know how much you love cars," said Marianne, trailing a finger across her chin.

"Will you drive?" he asked.

"Not allowed, I'm afraid." She exhaled, leaning her head back.

"Don't you miss the freedom of your old life?"

"I miss *walking*. Like literally walking to the supermarket to pick up a toothbrush. The U.S.? Not so much. I'm big on adventure." She got up and stretched her arms.

"How much longer are you here for?" he asked.

"Could be a day, could be a decade! Not up to me."

"I'll drive your car, if it's okay with you. Just this once."

"Hmmm."

"That buffoon guard of yours can follow us."

"Mmmmm," she said, twirling on her feet. "Do I detect a hint of jealousy?"

"He's very protective of you."

"He's here for my security. That's all."

"Are you sure?"

"Of course!" She pulled him by the hands. "Let's dance."

"Stayin' Alive" had begun playing on Marianne's phone. Javed stared at her.

Then his shoulders shimmied while his feet remained perfectly still. His forearms flicked and unlocked. The right hand rose skyward, finger erect, his hip thrust gorgeously to the left. He danced a pointy-finger dance. He spun on his feet and landed on a seamless toe stand.

Marianne grabbed him and kissed him on the lips. "Spend the night today. I don't know when we'll get the chance again."

"What do you mean?"

"I'm really happy to be with you and I want you to stay. And I *want to be able to say that.*"

"Of course. I've always wanted that, Marianne." He pulled her by the hands beyond the veranda and into the rain, where her face, streaked with rain, flushed a sultry freckled red.

On Sunday afternoon as Javed was shaving shirtless in front of the sink, his phone vibrated on the terrazzo countertop.

*"Haan jee!"* Javed pressed the speakerphone button.

His producer said he wanted to talk to Javed about something important. It would be best, he said, if they met in person. Javed said he would be happy to meet immediately, since he was busy in the evening.

Javed showered and changed and drove, his car zigzagging through the black-and-yellow concrete barriers, onto the main road, and on toward the studio headquarters of Jeet TV. He walked into a harshly lit meeting room with yellow chairs and a long beige table. His producer, Ahmed, in khakis and a denim shirt, met him inside. They hugged, and Ahmed tapped his hand to his heart. After asking Javed how he was, and whether he'd like some tea, he told Javed that the rating of Javed's show had dropped. He wasn't sure why, he said: the channel had monitored the rating for a month, and instead of climbing up, it had dipped. He told Javed, taking long pauses in between his words, that the channel had decided to shift Javed's show to the 3:00 p.m. slot.

A wave of distress plowed into Javed. The 3:00 p.m. slot was given to second-rate anchors and watched by housewives. He recognized a demotion when he saw one.

"I see," said Javed. "This is news to me."

He knew it would make no sense to share his concerns with a junior producer—a twenty-seven-year-old kid—like Ahmed.

To register his displeasure, which he knew would be reported to senior management, he added that the decision felt very sudden, and strange. He told Ahmed he would get back to him.

When Javed told Marianne the news over dinner at a Chinese restaurant, she tipped her head. "How do you feel?

"Bloody upset," he said, sliding to one side the chopsticks he couldn't use. "Feel cheated."

The restaurant was small, bathed in red and black tones. The ceiling was strung with illuminated red lanterns.

"Ask them to show you the numbers," she said. "Don't leave the slot without having seen the numbers."

"It's so bizarre. My show is one of the most popular. There's something fishy going on."

"Are you surprised?" she asked. "Did you have a sense of how the show was going?"

"Absolutely fine," said Javed. "As far as I know. My interview with the Chief Minister had the highest rating recently."

She placed her hand over his. "You'll be fine."

"I want to get to the bottom of this," he said.

"You absolutely must. And I'm here for you. Let me know how I can help." From the small bamboo steamer she pinned a dumpling between her chopsticks. "Try this, they're so good." Javed leaned over and she slipped the dumpling into his mouth.

Two days later a sanitation team in white uniform arrived to fix the pipes in Javed's house. Marianne had sent three Pakistanis, and an American supervised them. Javed was touched by the gesture. It hinted at a subtle intimacy, one that asked no questions but took liberties with its love.

Javed watched the men as they went about their work soundlessly. When he offered to pay, the American supervisor said the bill had been taken care of.

Javed went to the local florist and bought a large bouquet of imported lilies. He picked up a bottle of wine from his house. He'd never anticipated responding so readily to a woman's needs.

At the gate, the guard stopped him.

"You should know me by now, buddy."

"How can I help you?"

Javed told the guard to pat him down quickly so he could see Marianne.

A pink-orange sky stirred behind rows of swollen cloud.

The guard said Marianne Almond had left.

"What do you mean *left*?"

"She's gone back to the U.S."

The guard said she'd left Pakistan the night before. A new officer was due to move in.

Javed stood still, not sure if he had heard right. He knew he had heard right. A hot rushing pressure rose in his chest.

"But why?" he finally asked.

"You'll have to ask her that."

Javed stood on the pavement, trying to suppress the panic lashing inside him.

"I see," he said, and turned back.

In his bedroom Javed opened up his laptop and wrote Marianne an email. He typed an anguished note—How could she just leave without saying goodbye? What was going on? Was she planning on returning?—and deleted it. He typed a cooler note—Why had she left? Had something happened?—and deleted it. With a woman like Marianne, confrontation would not get him far. In the few weeks he'd known her, he'd learnt that resolute cheerfulness and candor—a strange combination— worked best with Marianne. Her own temperament was a mix of the two, and she'd demanded the same of her lover. As he fought back his tears, he thanked her, first, for having had the pipes fixed. He told her he'd walked over to her house to find her gone. He said he missed her terribly. He said he wished she'd told him about her departure. Why hadn't she told him?

Was she planning on returning?

As soon as Javed sent the email, he received an automated reply. Marianne Almond, the text said, would be away from her email for the next two weeks. It was her personal email address. The message didn't say more.

Javed coiled onto his bed, summoned by a sticky ache in his heart. A gusty rain swept Islamabad, showering leaves in his driveway. It carried away dust, glittering the trees and bushes. Marianne had told him that rain in Minneapolis made her blue, but the thundering Islamabad rains always gladdened her. It was impressions like these, so removed from his expectations of a foreign sensibility, which made her unique. He had marveled at her ease, her interest in his land and his people. Or perhaps she had said these things to impress him. Well-traveled people made masterful liars. As the rain slashed against his window, Javed imagined being killed. A scenario composed itself in his head: a group of terrorists would get past the barricade while Javed was out for a walk. They would kill him, and the Americans would retaliate. Javed would become a martyr, and Marianne Almond, cut up by relief that she'd escaped, and a very American guilt that Javed had not, would start a fund in his name. Old clips from his show would be played on TV. "A crusader on the screen. A hero in life." Marianne would feel wretched for having deserted him.

Javed looked out the window; the sky was a glinting pane, blue-gray, after a storm.

He wished desperately to cover the ground of his pain as fast as his body would allow. To muffle the wound for the time it took to forget it. It was how someone like him got by.

That night, Javed emptied a bottle of wine in the kitchen sink and watched with grim focus as the liquid slunk down the drain. The splash of red-purple filled him with despair. Without feeling coerced or pressured, he'd fallen in love. It wasn't an idealized past he missed, but the real encounters of intimacy—the jointly created jokes in which they'd sought sanctuary, the exchanging and shedding of vulnerability in their homes. She'd managed to pull him up from above, helping him become a more secure version of himself, at once holding him, comforting him from below.

He wished Marianne were standing next to him, pleading with him to not break the bottles. She would hold his arm and he would prop her up on the sink and fuck her.

From the kitchen window, Javed saw a new officer, perhaps Marianne's replacement, getting out of a black bulletproof SUV. She was a small woman with a mousy face and small shoulders. She tottered on high heels. She didn't touch, in passing, the hands and shoulders of her colleagues, as Marianne used to do.

He sprinted out of his kitchen, toward the gate, and up to the SUV.

"Javed Rehman." He plunged his hand forward. "Your neighbor." He pointed to his house.

"Hello, Javed. Vicky Shields."

"Welcome, Miss Shields. Excuse the intrusion, but any idea why Marianne Almond left so suddenly?"

"Not at liberty to say. I'm sorry." Her face froze. And she turned on her heels.

"One moment!" said Javed. But her security guards indicated, their palms out, that he should stay away.

Though Javed had retreated to the sofa, to the churning darkness offered by his eyes, sleep eluded him. He flipped and tossed. No matter how hard he pressed his eyes shut, the mind chugged.

Javed ignored the many phone calls from his producer asking him where he was, what he'd decided, and, finally, if he was alive.

When he arrived at the home of his former in-laws to meet Inaya, Sameena came by to say hello. Javed apologized for not having shown up for four weeks.

"We were wondering what happened," said Sameena, a hand on her hip. "Bachelor life too hectic?"

"I'm sorry," he said. "I'm really sorry." His voice was rough, dispatched from a place deeper than his vocal cords.

He placed his phone on the table in front of him. He picked up Inaya, inhaling her tart, powdery scent. Sameena sat down on the sofa next to the door.

"I need to see Inaya more often," he said.

"Just look at the bags under your eyes."

"I just. Please. Twice a week." He kissed Inaya's belly.

"Once a week is more than enough if you can be bothered to make it."

"You can send her to my house if you prefer."

"Absolutely out of the question." Sameena flicked the hair out of her eyes. "Your house is a hovel. Just stepping inside gives one depression."

"I promise it's clean now. I clean it myself sometimes."

"If you're going to lie about stupid things, I'm not letting my child near you."

"I'm not, but fine. I'm really not. I'll come here to see her."

His phone lit up. The locked screen showed the first line of the email. Javed heaved himself toward the phone, handing Inaya to her mother.

*Hi—great to hear from you. Sorry for late reply—just arrived in Sierra Leone. And sorry not to have said a real goodbye! Left in a rush. Am working in the countryside, not checking email regularly. Yrs, MA.*

He read Marianne's email twice. The first time his heart surged so loudly he could barely focus on the words. He read it again, taking in the more helpful aspects of the information she'd provided. He imagined Marianne in a green field, brushing hair off the foreheads of strangers' children. The thought of her walking around in her cotton tunic, her breasts safe and fragrant, steadied him. He read the email for the third time, registering her heartbreaking reserve. He wondered why she had signed off so formally, with her initials.

His eyes mapped the text.

*Yrs, MA*

*Yrs, Mini Apple*

He looked up from the phone and saw Sameena staring at him. He sat down next to her and, his hands hanging by his sides, gazed blankly forward.

# Breezy Blessings

How many girls from good families have gone into this line of work? I'm not the type of mother who says, 'Sit at home.' But do something decent I say. Now look at your sister."

"I'll marry whomever you want me to marry," Mehak said.

"All day I'll be left alone with this useless man," her mother said, unafraid of her wounding candor about her own husband, who sat at the edge of the sofa stirring sugar into his tea. Mehak's father did not look up.

Afterward, he went to Mehak's room and took her hand in his own. Mehak looked at his hand, strewn with black wisps of sideswept hair. He smiled, and told her not to worry: it was her first lead role, and there was no doubt in his mind she should take it. One day, when she won Best Actress at the Jeet TV Awards, *he* would give the speech.

"I love you, Abbu *jaan*," she told him.

She returned the director's call as her father looked on.

"It sounds perfect, sir," she said on the phone. "I'm over the moon. I've been a fan of yours for sooooo long." She tapped the speakerphone button.

"So sweet of you. And feeling is totally mutual. I wanted someone sweet, even little bit shy. The story is little violent. Nothing serious. Just a few slaps."

Mehak said it would be her honor. She looked at her father and shrugged.

⁓

TWO WEEKS LATER, in a large apartment complex by the name of Breezy Blessings, Roshan tipped a tray before Mehak. "VIP chai for you, moonface." He lifted his shoulder in a shy heave and laughed, his own words a thrill, a tickle.

Roshan's fitted T-shirt and denim bell-bottoms made him look like an overgrown boy, which Mehak supposed he was, considering he was twenty-one. His eyelashes dipped and curled and seemed to smash up against the glass of his purple spectacles.

The anticipation of Roshan's teasing grin, the taste of Lipton Yellow Label whipped with powdered milk, had become the high point of Mehak's day: a gracious ceremony between two people who'd met just a few days before. Unlike the rest of the crew, who treated Mehak as if she were a gnat in a well-oiled machine, Roshan had conferred an *aap* upon her the moment they'd been introduced. This gesture of respect, as gentle as it was solemn, had touched Mehak more than she could say. She was, after all, a year older.

The same evening, as Mehak stepped into the ironing room to retrieve her clothes, she pulled herself back: Roshan was leaning into a boy. His lips grazed the boy's ear and his chin hovered, as if depositing a secret—or a kiss.

Mehak hadn't imagined Roshan's life beyond the churn of

duty: running in and out of rooms replenishing cups of chai, bottled water, reused makeup sponges glistening with soap.

Mehak swiveled around and, in her nervousness, shut the door behind her with utmost respect.

Roshan yanked open the door and stepped outside.

Mehak looked him in the eye. "I didn't see a thing."

The stranger bolted.

Roshan opened his mouth, his eyelashes rippling in panic.

Mehak said: "Won't say a thing. Didn't see a thing."

"If you didn't see a thing, why are you telling me you didn't see a thing? I know the type of girl you are. I know you're seeing *everything*."

"No!"

"My heart beats fifty-two times a minute. Every time with the permission of Allah."

She blinked, hoping to invite a revelation of some sort.

"When a baby is thrown into the crib for the first time, the direction in which his feet fall tells the mother the direction her son will walk for the rest of his life: left or right." A vein rose on Roshan's forehead. "My feet fell to the left. *So now you're going to judge me?*" He glared at her. "My mother is my life. Everyone else I don't care about."

"Please understand—"

"Last night a stranger messaged me saying my family doesn't love me because it's *haram* to love me. I got so upset I uploaded a photo of myself without a shirt. Lots of 'likes' came. Then I was relax."

"I promise I won't say anything," said Mehak. "That was the point I was trying to make. I don't care what you do in your private life."

He looked at her suspiciously. "Promise to Allah?"

"Promise. To Allah."

After the director shouted "Pack up!" at the ceiling fan at 11:00 p.m., Roshan communicated to Mehak with a coy pinch of the eyes that he had something to say. She was unsure what to make of the overture, but she met him again in the ironing room, and he held her chin as a grandmother would a child's: "Like to smoke, angel?"

Mehak giggled. "Sometimes." (She'd smoked a cigarette once.)

The crew were clattering out of the hallway, dragging away lights as tall as cupboards.

Roshan took Mehak by the arm, down the whitewashed stairs of Breezy Blessings, to a stone bench surrounded by trees and shrubs and the dull fizz of mosquitoes. There he lit up, took a long relishing drag, and passed the cigarette to Mehak. She held it between thumb and forefinger. She coughed when she inhaled; Roshan rubbed her back and prized the cigarette from her.

He recommended she begin by not inhaling; one day, she'd inhale without knowing it, he said, and it would be a spectacular feeling.

He confessed that he used bottled water in her tea, tap water in everyone else's.

Mehak was smiling, but she longed to ask Roshan: Who was the boy in the ironing room? She knew that an unspoken decorum barred the exchange of intimacies. The two older actresses on set had already begun monitoring—subtly, they seemed to think—Mehak's conversations with the male staff. Both women swept their hair into glossy brown buns and made sure, at least once a week, to declare the tea not hot enough. "We want it scalding," they'd say. "Scalding!" And they would glower, and grin. Each time they protested, the director scolded Roshan for not looking after his "senior artists." Mehak envied the frugality of their verse, their way of assigning meaning through sly inflections of agreement (*hmmm*) or rebuke (hmm).

"I never told you," said Roshan, drawing on his cigarette and flexing his long, arched foot above the grass. "On your first day, when you had gone to the bathroom and someone else was reading your lines, the cameraman told the hero, 'For the right eyeline, just pretend Mehak is that stain on the wall.'"

Everyone, Roshan reported, had sniggered.

"Including Sabina?" Mehak asked.

"She was the first to laugh."

Mehak reminded herself, again, that Sabina Malik, not quite a senior artist, nor a junior like Mehak, was only three years older. She seemed wiser, a woman who understood the compact allure of her body. The tighter the *kameez* the more her personality seemed to come alive. Sabina wore hair extensions that were dispatched every morning to be ironed along with her wardrobe. When she needed a favor she yelped in a baby voice.

Roshan turned to Mehak. "I really like you but you're a shy girl. With a God-killing smile. But shy. How come you wanted to act?"

How to put into words that once the camera came on, a warm fire rose from within?

She became the girl from Nazimabad who had the power to do exactly as she was doing now: sneaking a cigarette on a crowded set.

"I just love it," she said, laying her palms flat on the stone bench, looking up at the muggy, twinkly sky.

.

The next day Mehak arrived at Breezy Blessings straight from the salon to shoot a wedding scene. She'd had her long hair blown out and streaked. Mehak had wanted something with a tinge of caramel, but the beautician had insisted on a lighter shade. The color now matched the hair of child beggars—a rust-yellow dyed by the sun. Sitting in the makeup room on a swiveling chair drenched in cigarette ash, holding a strand of beggar-blond hair in her fist, Mehak looked at Roshan, then in the mirror, miming an expression of disgust. Roshan reassured her that the Pakistani TV screen had not seen anything like her hair color. She looked like a Turkish soap star.

He offered her a cup of chai. "A Turkish star who sadly keeps her cleavage covered." He huffed: "You're more beautiful than Sabina. *By the way.*"

"And you're a liar. Everyone loves her."

"The first thing you need to learn is to stop complimenting your rivals. You'll get nowhere." Roshan licked his lips impatiently: "Color of bridal dress?"

"Whatever the director wants."

"My wife wore maroon on our wedding. Stupid cow. You must wear silver."

"Your wife?"

"What's that look on your face?"

"I thought you liked—"

"I like all of God's creations it's *imperative* to like all of God's creations what does being married have to do with anything *uff* what am I going to do with this girl."

"Relax," said Mehak. "I was just asking."

"Relax," said Roshan. "I was just explaining."

He blew a strand of hair off his face. "I got a tattoo."

He flipped his arm. The tattoo read, *I HATE MY LIFE.*
"Huh?"

"Everyone is stopping to ask, 'Are you okay, Roshan?'"

"Sorry to say but you've gone *craz-yyy!*" laughed Mehak, swirling the tea in her mouth. "Like totally and completely *mad.*"

"You're an actress but about drama you know *nothing.* I'll have to teach you everything. So many comments coming on my page. Asking if I'm fine. Or sad or alone. If I need anything. I feel *so much* loved."

Roshan retrieved the empty cups of tea—from the carpet, from inside the bottom drawer of the makeup dresser—and skipped out the door just as the makeup artist, a woman of about forty, walked in.

She was keen to get started: a heroine's tardiness wound up being, always, the makeup artist's fault. She surveyed Mehak's face with sullen disinterest and squirted a glistening blob of liquid foundation onto her palm. She tapped a portly finger, dripping with the makeup, onto Mehak's forehead, nose, and cheeks. Mehak clamped her eyelids shut as a finger prodded them to determine the strength of her fake eyelashes. With her knee the makeup artist spun the chair to face the mirror, violently parting Mehak's hair with a tail comb.

In the early evening, under a beige arch that led to the garden, the crew carried a velvet sofa onto a scaffold of wooden slats. It was windy outside, a relief from the afternoon scorch, when the "senior artists" had continued to demand scalding tea even as shards of sun pierced through the curtainless makeup room. Mehak breathed in, she breathed out. She had read the script the night before: a short wedding montage, outdoors, followed by a scene in the bedroom when her husband would slap her for the first time.

Mehak was grateful for the way Karachi slackened as the sky turned gray, a hazy shuffle of cloud and sea. She walked into the garden holding her floor-length skirt a few inches above her ankles, as if wading through a puddle. The wind slammed and turned. One of Mehak's fake eyelashes drooped, and her hand flew to her eye, pressing the lash into place. She squinted as she rehearsed her most important piece of dialogue. *It may be okay to fall in other people's estimation, but I never want to fall in my own.* She didn't have a long monologue. If she was slapped hard enough, if she responded with real tears, she would quickly become a household name.

On each side of the velvet sofa the crew had placed floor candelabras. The trees had been strung with roses, the ghostly trunks of the eucalyptus made disco-yellow with light. A dozen extras milled around, chatting with one another; Mehak's costar, Sohail, was crossing the garden toward her, smiling.

Then the director arrived: he shouted for order, lit a cigarette, snapped his fingers at the crew. He was a tall, bald man whose starched *shalwar kameez* rustled against his body.

"A quick camera rehearsal, then we ROLL!" he announced.

Sohail greeted Mehak warmly as he sat down on the sofa.

Mehak adjusted the folds of her dress.

"Looking pretty," said Sohail.

"Not as good as you." Mehak smiled.

"Quite humid, no?"

"What do you expect, it's Karachi."

"CUE FOR CAMERA REHEARSAL!"

Sohail leaned forward on the sofa and whispered his opening line to Mehak.

The director was watching his actors on a monitor placed before him on the grass.

Sohail rested his palm on Mehak's right cheek, and brought his lips to her left.

Mehak jerked her neck back.

"Sir, I—I—can't do this," she said from the stage of wooden slats.

"It's not a French kiss," said the director.

Mehak had vowed she would never kiss on-screen—cheek, nose, neck. With that pledge from Mehak, her father had been able to calm her mother: their daughter would set her own rules.

"I'm not feeling one hundred percent comfortable, sir," said Mehak. "My mother will not like it."

"Listen, girl," said the director as he strode up to the stage. "The only reason I want to show physical contact is because you don't know how to flirt."

"But I do, sir."

"Stand up."

She lifted the folds of her heavily embroidered skirt. She gripped the candelabra as she stood up.

"Show me, then. Show me how to do Romance with big R."

Mehak tilted her head to the side and summoned a wistful look in her eyes. The expression around her mouth remained uncertain, like a grimace.

"Pth-thaatic!" said the director.

The three camera gaffers—one of whom had been rolling his snot into a ball on his palm—sat up.

"Sir, leave it," Sohail said. "There's a slap later anyway, so this scene can be done without kissing."

"*Especially* because of the slap, you *must* be shown to be giddy at this moment. Have you idiots not read the script?"

Mehak looked at the lighting technician, a boy of seventeen. He was staring plaintively at her breasts.

She took a quick breath. "It's fine. I mean cheek should be fine, right?" She wasn't sure whom she had asked the question.

"Are you sure?" responded Sohail.

Mehak nodded.

"Give us a minute, sir."

"This is not a Hollywood film, hero. I don't have this kind of free time."

"Just one minute, sir."

"Are you sure your parents will be okay with this?" Sohail whispered.

"I don't know, but I don't want him to be angry at me. Let's do this before he gets even more angry."

"As you say."

Mehak raised her hand to acknowledge she was ready.

"Roll the fucking camera. It seems our stars have decided they want to work," said the director.

She was light-headed. Her neck burned.

As soon as the shoot ended Mehak changed out of her bridal outfit into a pair of jeans and a T-shirt. With a tissue she mauled the red lipstick off her mouth. As she hurried out of Breezy Blessings she heard a voice behind her: "Allah puts those in pain who He loves the *most*." Roshan had been instructed to stay in the kitchen when the camera rolled, but he always lingered for Mehak's scenes, often crouching behind a large plant, bribing one of the crew boys with a mouth freshener that doubled as a mild stimulant.

Jogging up to her, zipping his faux-leather jacket, Roshan said, "Do happy people turn to Allah? Never. Sad ones are his special ones because they're always seeking His help." He touched her shoulder with a slack tap. "Like you and me."

"I don't want to talk about you right now." She peeled off her fake eyelashes, wincing where the glue was firm.

"I'm serious." His eyes skimmed the floor. "The pain is for special people."

"Everyone here is selfish," Mehak said. "They don't care about the actors. They just want the right shot." She got into the car and slammed the door.

The white Suzuki Alto sped along the charred asphalt. Billboards of models looking glum and imperial loomed above overpasses, in the foreground of traffic signals. Multiplexes smeared the skyline. Everywhere Mehak looked, Karachi leaked nighttime neon: *Tipu Burger & Broast, Baloch Ice Cream, Nihari Inn*.

Mehak wound down the window; the plastic handle came off in her hand. She looked at it with a sigh.

"Your handle is broken!" She waved it in the rearview mirror.

"Many things are broken. This road is broken. The upcoming traffic light is broken." He drove with one hand; his elbow stuck out the window. "Just leave it on the seat," he said listlessly.

Long before Mehak had first sat in the Alto, she'd imagined what it would mean to arrive on set in a chauffeur-driven car. She'd searched Sabina's fan page on the Internet and had lingered, with fretting intensity, on her photos. A black-and-white shot showed Sabina in a luxurious car, gazing out of the window, her lips coldly puckered.

Back in her room Mehak heard a sharp *ding* from inside her handbag. She clawed out her phone.

"Sorry about what happened today."

It was the first time the director had texted her.

"No problem, sir," she wrote back.

"It was a stressful day for everyone."

"True," she typed back.

"I'm outside your house."

She stared at the screen of her phone.

Her parents were asleep.

She ran down the stairs, her bag slung on her shoulder, and opened the gate of the house.

She spoke quickly as he slid down the passenger window. "Sir, please don't take any stress."

"I feel so embarrassed," he said, leaning over toward the open window. "I'm really sorry, *beta*."

"It's all right, sir. Tempers are short on set."

But he'd already pushed open the door for her.

"Are you sure you've forgiven me?" he asked as she climbed into the car. "There's so much pressure from the producer to shoot this damn thing ASAP. But I really need to get my temper under control. I'm trying."

"Sir, please. We all respect you."

"I'm glad we're good. Please don't call me 'sir.' What do you want to eat? In the mood for a party? Full of youngsters like you."

She asked him what kind of party it was.

He said it was like all the others.

She didn't exactly know what other parties were like.

They parked outside a white house with a looming wooden gate. Coils of barbed wire sat evenly on the high walls, like a wraparound bracelet.

A security guard escorted the director in and Mehak followed him, stretching her T-shirt over her belly.

She found herself in a spacious room full of bare legs, cigarette smoke, and silver lights stuttering from hidden depths. Mehak had seen women in dresses on social media and she had often wished to be them. Seeing them in the flesh, she felt an indistinct concern.

She gazed at a woman in a spangled silver dress. As the woman turned around to face Mehak, the smell of liquor sprang from her mouth. In her high heels and sturdy milky calves, she seemed unaware of her own terrible exposure.

"THIS IS MEHAK," the director shouted over the shattering music. "She's playing the second lead in my new serial." Mehak smiled and shook hands with the woman. Her collarbones were so deep they could rock a baby to sleep.

Her eyes ranged over Mehak. "Pretty girl."

A waiter brought Mehak a glass of wine and Mehak held it with both hands, as if it were a hot drink.

The woman scuttled forward. "Your face tells me you don't imbibe. Yes?" She smiled impishly, at once perceiving and pitying Mehak's condition. She flicked a shred of dry lipstick from the corner of her lip. "Chill the fuck out," she said. "I'm not here to judge." And she staggered into the darkness.

Mehak looked around and saw silken shoulders and men in ironed polo shirts. In the corner of the room a famous model crouched on the floor, in a short skirt, retrieving bits of broken glass.

Mehak walked up to the bar and exchanged her wine for a glass of water. She drank it thirstily.

She found the director in the alcove under the stairs, a speck of powder in his left nostril. "Sweet, sweet Mehak," he said, wiping his nose.

"*Chalein,* sir. I'm ready. Shoot starts early tomorrow."

"How right you are! Let's leave," he sniffed. "Letsgoletsgo letsgo!"

"Sir, I can call a taxi."

"Don't be silly. I shall drop you." They passed into a steamy chamber with an indoor pool, and Mehak saw that the woman with the clavicles had jumped in. Her mascara had run, she looked confused, and as she paddled to the shallow end of the pool, a knot of guests chuckled.

"Ice cream?" asked the director as they got into his SUV. "Sorry the party was so boring."

"Not boring!" said Mehak, meaning it. "So many characters," she smiled.

"You see, what I *like* about you is that you're genuinely a good kid."

The scent of cigarettes curled around the dashboard, the wheel, his shirt.

He drove to a roadside kiosk, around which a swarm of cars had collected, and ordered two choco-bars. Two teenage boys jogged back and forth from the single bald bulb of the shop to the crumbling headlight beams of the cars. A boy in a green T-shirt darted toward the car, an applicator sponge in his hand. The director indicated "no" with his finger, but the boy, accustomed to such mild-mannered dismissal, splashed soapy arcs across the windshield, wiping them with the blade on the other side of his sponge. He grinned and was nudged aside by the peon who'd brought ice cream. The director extended his hand. The money was quickly plucked. The feet retreated.

"I love the yellow vanilla inside," said the director. "Ever since I was a child. It's so hard to find nowadays."

"Ditto, sir. Same!" She tore open the ice cream.

"Every time you call me 'sir' I feel like a seventy-year-old uncle." He smiled as he reversed the car. "Don't be so formal. Just Shahaab. Eat it, or it'll melt."

"Yes, sir." She blinked. "Sorry! Sorry!"

She laughed. He chuckled gloomily.

She slid a cracked peak of chocolate onto her tongue, and into her mouth.

"Acting is all about the eyes. Now say my name softly. At the same time say it with complete confidence."

She whispered his name in a low voice, looking at him.

"Not bad."

The roads were wide and clear and blue.

"Nice car," she said.

"Ten years of my savings." He sighed. "But what an honor to have such a pretty girl sitting in it." He placed a hand on her thigh. "My friend at the party was saying as well. Most actresses don't have the kind of screen presence you have at such a young age. It's the eyes. Are they from Mama or Papa?"

"I think—Abbu."

He rolled his knuckles over her jeans. "*MashaAllah*. Always say *MashaAllah*."

She drew her leg away.

"Learn how to take a compliment," he snapped.

She looked straight ahead.

He cleared his throat. "I want to help you, Mehak."

Frozen, she looked ahead. The car was moving, moving.

"When Sabina came to me, she was loud and vulgar and

cheap. People used to laugh at her behind her back. Look at her now. Doing all the lead roles."

It was true that Sabina was rarely seen to be angry, tailoring even her grievances into a play of coquetry.

"Do you trust me?" he asked.

Mehak nodded, her gaze tacked to the curve of the road.

"Do you have hopes and dreams or do you want to play the lead's sister for the rest of your life?"

"Hopes and dreams." The ice cream had soaked her fingers.

"Good. Just a little lost. I will groom you. By thirty it's over for a woman. The next few years are crucial for you. You get me? You have to keep your circle tight. Know who's looking out for you, who's not. You get me?"

"Yes, sir."

The car rolled to a stop outside her house.

"Do you know how to say anything other than 'yes, sir'?"

*"Allah Hafiz."*

She took care to walk slowly—the ice-cream stick pinched in her hand—to show she was ambling, she was perfectly fine.

Mehak gripped the edges of the bathroom sink. Hadn't she recently heard one of the country's most sought-after actresses discuss, on a morning show, her early humiliations, and how they had sharpened her? The actress had said she wore her scars as badges of honor. The audience had clapped.

For the first time, with a twist of sadness, Mehak understood what the actress meant: to be a good actor was to brutishly woo your own, most useful, emotions. *Especially* offscreen. It was to make a pact with yourself that the job came before—and would withstand—the small treacheries detected by the heart.

*But it was all so predictable:* the degradation on set followed by an apology followed by a party—

On set the next morning, Mehak remembered to relax her facial muscles. She threw her shoulders back.

When she tried to catch Roshan's eye, to see if he'd noticed the tautness about her, she saw him tailing a handsome journalist who'd arrived to interview the cast.

After lunch, the director's assistant walked over to Mehak in the makeup room. She was sitting on the floor, in front of an open suitcase, sifting through the wardrobe she carried with her to set, and back, every day.

He scratched his head with a pen. "We are not doing any scenes with you today. Sabina boss is priority. She is going to USA next week."

Mehak looked up. "Why did you ask me to come today?"

The assistant lifted his arm in a shrug. "Sometimes confusion happens." He held the script in his other hand.

"And tomorrow?"

"Tomorrow's schedule is unclear."

"The day after?"

"Unclear, lady. Everything is unclear."

"But you're shooting with Sabina?"

"How many times do I have to tell you she's going to USA?"

"I have four scenes with her in episode two," Mehak said softly. "That's why I was asking."

"Those scenes have been cut." He ran his thumb along the spiral binding of the script. "Cut. Cut. Cut. According to the new script."

She looked at him. "What *new* script?"

"We will update you."

"Update me about *what*?"

"Some things have changed. Some roles have changed. Let's see what happens."

Her heart raced.

The assistant was already out the door, and she felt tears spring to her eyes. She wiped them with the back of her hand, kneeling in front of the cupboard where her makeup was stored.

Mehak scrunched her *shalwars* and lobbed them into the suitcase.

She heard the clip of Sabina's kitten heels behind her. "You look stressed today," said Sabina.

Mehak continued packing, determined not to turn her face around. She could see Sabina from the corner of her eye.

Sabina wound her petite, buxom body on the makeup chair and exhaled. "Don't mind it," she said, surveying her face in a handheld mirror. "But your acting has been constipated." A finger grazed her chin for ingrown hair. "Even Sir said."

"What did he say?"

"Just between you and me. But he said some things."

"What things?"

"Well." She yanked an offender from her chin with yellow tweezers. "He took me to the side and said, 'Have you noticed? She's a bad performer. There's no other way to put it.'"

"In those words?"

"His exact words. The expressions are coming out wooden, babe. Have you looked at yourself on the monitor? You should see yourself on the monitor. If you have a question, just ask. What do you think these joker assistants are there for?" A tinkling laugh rose from her throat. "It's showbiz, *na*. You have to look like Deepika, work like a donkey, think like a man." She rubbed her lips together, smacked them. "And pray. You *have* to pray. I've never seen you pray. Sad."

Mehak nodded, looking into the pool of clothes, bloodlike before her tears.

Outside the gate, in the scattered dust of the afternoon, Roshan stood under a parched willowy palm drinking a can of Coca-Cola and smoking a cigarette.

"Madam Mehak!" He squashed the cigarette under his foot.

Mehak dipped her head to hide her choked face.

She handed him her phone. "Can you please call me an Uber?"

"Can you please look up?"

She crumpled the tissue in her hand.

"Oh God. Look at your face. Tell me what happened."

"Can you do as I'm saying?"

"I'm not going to let you go like this. Who made you cry?"

She shook her head. "I got cut." Her voice cracked. "From the project."

*"Oh God."* He clasped her fingers. "How do you know?"

"He sent his little sidekick to tell me."

"I've been with this crew for four years. Seen more than you can imagine. Motherfucker. You must go live on Insta. Right now. I've had enough."

"Are you crazy?"

"I'm turning on the video. Just stay like this. Trust me. Talk to your fans. *Right now.*"

"I don't have many . . . fans."

"After this you will. Tell them you got dropped but you're

not sure why. That's it. That's the line. Don't say more. You look *perfect*."

"I don't want to lie," she said flatly.

"Tomorrow we tell the truth. Try to understand." He gritted his teeth and flung his gaze to the gate. "They'll call me back inside *any* minute."

He held up her phone. "Are you ready? I'm turning on the video! Three—two—one: Okay, you're LIVE."

Her eyes were red, muddled. She looked steadily at the screen until they pooled with feigned tears.

# A Life of Its Own

## Part One

As the Prado SUV swept up the dirt road to the three-hundred-year-old *haveli,* an attendant leapt to open the door for a philanthropist couple from London—important guests today of Syeda Zareena Bokhari.

ZB stepped out of the SUV in sunglasses, a *chaadar* ordered over her hair.

Kashif and Farah crawled out from the back of the car.

Mansoor, the manager of the *haveli,* garlanded Jon Willoughby with a necklace of silver tinsel and thousand-rupee notes. Maintaining a distance, arms outstretched, he hung a necklace of five-hundred-rupee notes on Jon's wife, Cynthia. Though Mansoor had arranged the gifts, Farah knew he could have done so only after ZB's approval. ZB's flighty, recreational treachery no longer jolted Farah. In a pretense of moral harmony, it was her mother-in-law who often seemed eager to please her staff, accommodating within herself sudden quicksilver hypocrisies and remaining, as a matter of principle, blind to her own quirks. Last month ZB had helped her maid get an abortion; the week before ZB had dissuaded a different maid from a divorce because her spouse happened to be ZB's trusted old gardener.

"Welcuhm, welcuhm," ZB murmured to the Willoughbys as she herded all before her, sending a band of attendants scurrying into the house.

Many in the crowd wanted to accompany ZB inside; they were shooed away by Mansoor's long, thin arms. The doors of the *haveli,* made of ancient *shisham* and secured with an iron latch chain, thudded behind Farah.

"Scratchy!" Jon laughed, fingering the prickly tinsel garland.

"Let me take that from you." Kashif smiled at Jon, helping him remove the garland.

Farah remembered the first time she'd visited Maujpur, three months before, during her wedding festivities. Kashif's face had been pinched with angst as he and Farah walked through a shower of rose petals. "It's a monumental lie," Kashif had said, lightly dodging the soggy petals.

"What is?" Farah had asked, smiling through the flowers.

"All of this," he'd said, sketching the air, not knowing where to begin.

ZB—as Zareena Bokhari had instructed Farah to call her, she loathed "aunty"—had shown Farah the jasmine vines, the pomegranate trees, referring to them as "*my* trees and plants."

Now catching her breath in the central courtyard of the *haveli,* surrounded by a wall of mosaic tiles twinkling with heat, Farah thought of the startling direction in which her life had slid: she and Kashif were to move to Manhattan right after the wedding. It was where Kashif, an attorney, had built a home for himself.

But a week after Farah and Kashif's wedding, as ZB got into the Prado for Maujpur, the family's ancestral hometown three hours south of Lahore, she slumped into the seat with a surge of nausea and pain in her chest.

She survived the heart attack. She underwent bypass surgery. Kashif postponed the flight to New York by three weeks.

"Here I am trying to be positive," ZB had said then, clutching a pillow to her chest to cushion her ribs. "And look at the rest of you. Wimps!" She'd laughed croakily. "My food should be cooked in olive oil *only*."

Her daughters would fly in from London, and Dubai, if the need arose, ZB said, to look after her.

Privately, Kashif told Farah he'd decided to quit his job in New York: he was needed in Pakistan. His mother was getting on.

Farah, who had only rarely traveled outside of Pakistan, had dreamed of working in Manhattan, reporting for CNN or Vice. She'd dreamed, specifically, of traveling and broadcasting with a camera crew, merging her obsessive knowledge of South Asia with global politics. She'd pictured herself in a bright parka, her face cold-bitten but exultant—a journalist's face.

Slouched outside his mother's bedroom, Kashif had told Farah he was sorry, but they would have to build a life in Pakistan.

Farah would've accepted the apology had Kashif not added, tensely, that he was his parents' only son.

The Maujpur *haveli* was built upon an ancient mound dating all the way back to "God knows when," ZB was saying to Cynthia as she strode past the two-tiered, star-shaped marble fountain in the center of the courtyard. ZB talked of Kashif's paternal family as if it were her own, Farah had noticed. She had married into them, but Maujpur had come to be her turf, more than that of her husband, who, as a member of Parliament from the constituency of Maujpur, spent most of his time in Islamabad. ZB loved telling everyone that Syed Mahmood Mauj Darya Bokhari was the great love of her life.

In the reception room ZB's choice of food had the easy look of a fatty rural feast: chicken cooked in its own broth; *saag paneer* with corn *roti;* mutton kebabs off the spit; rice garnished with cilantro; Kabuli chickpeas and egg stew with a heap of chopped coriander, green chili, fried onion, and ginger. ZB pointed to the tablecloth. It was made of cotton grown on her land, she explained to the Willoughbys, spun on wheels by the women of Maujpur, many of whom were in her employ. Jon rubbed the rough cream cotton between his thumb and forefinger. "You have to smell it," said ZB. "It has a life of its own."

"How brilliant," murmured Jon, bending to sniff the cloth.

"It's always a delight to welcome British friends here," said ZB, as she took her seat at the head of the dark oak table. She wore a *shalwar kameez* of white paisley designs embroidered on salmon-pink cotton. A brief dip in her wrist sprang into a mound of arm.

"One has many fond memories of the Raj," she said.

A ripple puzzled across Cynthia's features.

"But I have to tell you," said ZB. "My uncle refused a knighthood because he was so swept up in the independence movement for Pakistan." She poured sweetened *lassi* into a brass goblet placed before Jon. "*Big* mistake." Her eyes lit up.

"Hah!" said Kashif. He turned to the Willoughbys. "It's just family myth. He was never offered it."

"Of course he was!" chided ZB. "There was a conspiracy by Gandhi to deprive him of it. But, as I said, it doesn't matter because the poor man never really wanted it, you see." She looked at Jon with a shudder of loving reproach. "How *wonderful* it would've been to have met the Queen."

"Mmmm," said Jon. "Ah, yes. The Queen."

"I've always wanted to see her jewelry up close."

"My mother," Kashif beamed tightly, "has a delightful knack for stories. And jewels. I'm a huge Ambedkar fan. Gandhi less so."

"Fascinating," said Jon.

"Gandhi went to great lengths to sabotage the Pakistan movement," said ZB. "One would have no identity without Pakistan. One would be just another demoralized Muslim in India."

"Instead one can be a demoralized Muslim in Pakistan!" chirped Kashif.

"He was immensely spoilt." ZB laughed, waving her hand about. "Anyhow, so glad he's returned to his home, his soil."

"How *wonderful,*" said Cynthia, sensing an opening. "A happy mummy!"

"Have you tried the corn *roti?*" asked ZB as she bit into the burnt round bread. Crumbs mobbed her waxy pink lipstick. "*All* organic. All made by my women."

"Corn. *Roti* . . . Mmmm . . ."

"Not a great idea to wear this *see-through* material in front of the male serfs." ZB suddenly turned to Farah. "It's lovely, but I can see your bra."

Farah colored as she looked at her *kameez*. The material was slightly translucent, but she'd made sure to drape a *dupatta* around her.

"Every inch of me is covered," said Farah. "And the word is 'house help.'" She smiled briskly at the Willoughbys.

"It's a reality, I tell you," said ZB, fanning herself with a cotton napkin. "This climate change business. It's *boiling*. And it's only September." A soupy film of talcum powder ringed her neck.

"Remember the good old days when the weather was small talk?" said Kashif, keen to press on.

"Exactly!" said Jon.

"Kashif," said ZB to her son. "You must extend your trip by four days until the formal inauguration of the community kitchen."

"Can't, Ma, can't, sadly!" said Kashif, with the jumpy, averting warmth of a son schooled by his mother's resolve. If one gave in to ZB the first time, Farah knew, one found oneself frequently detained.

"Farah has to get back to Lahore," said Kashif, with a late, zingy smile.

"For *God's sake*," said ZB. "These days all you need is a phone to be a journalist."

"I can't hold meetings on the phone," snapped Farah.

"Why don't you ask Saleem *mamoun*? He'll come running," said Kashif.

"One could, I suppose." ZB studied the wild roses on the rim of her Wedgwood plate. "My brother isn't the brightest bulb on the Christmas tree, you see," she explained to Jon. "A good man," she said with a thoughtful scowl. "But a man with the intelligence of a quilt."

"Ah!"

"He's loyal to you," said Kashif. "Wish I could say the same for your other brother."

"Correct," said ZB. "Thing is"—she looked acutely at Cynthia—"one's younger brothers were less capable than one. One was a person with promise, but that promise was snatched away to accommodate one's father's view of the world: there was black, and there was white; there were heirs, and there were spares."

*"Gosh!"*

"Eat. You must eat." ZB gestured to the array of food. "No wonder you're so svelte. You don't eat!"

"Not true!" Cynthia laughed; she blushed. "I have an *enormous* appetite," she said, and as Farah gazed at Cynthia's bird-like frame, it seemed to her she had exactly the opposite.

Farah looked fixedly at her own plate; she was marooned once again in the confident upper-class chaos of the world of her in-laws. A dull anger, a kind of yearning wrapped in mistrust, bubbled inside her. She removed the discolored lace doily from the silver tumbler before her and swigged back the sting of grapefruit juice. Her hand brushed against the gold chain on her neck to soothe her sense of her own worth.

She'd made a name for herself as a journalist, her peers respected her, *she respected herself*. But she would never exude, as Kashif did, the sleepy glimmer of wealth. It lived in her husband, in the drawl of his Punjabi, in his athletically veined arms. It bounced off the stretch of his shoulder. If he embraced it, he honored providence; if he repudiated it, he was gallant.

The day before, when Farah and Kashif had driven with ZB to Maujpur, Farah had noticed that ZB held Kashif's hand. As the Prado raced past the countryside, passing rows of eucalyptus, *keekar,* and, closer to Maujpur, mango orchards carved silver by the midday sun, ZB had stroked Kashif's hand, smiling at her son and heir.

⌐⁓

FROM ACROSS THE NEIGHBOR'S WALL a dog howled in the darkness. A firefly skirted the edge of a potted plant, flickered for a bright hot second, and merged with the stagnant night. At 9:00 p.m. Farah sat cross-legged on a rope-strung *charpai* in the third courtyard, away from ZB's quarters adjoining the central courtyard. She was smoking a cigarette, a hip flask tucked under her crossed legs, staring at the underwater light in the tiny fountain on the side of the brick enclosure. She thought of the first time she'd met Kashif, two years before, at a party in Lahore. At Farah's age, when a thoughtful-seeming man asked for her number, she shared it without being coy. The charm of being twenty-nine and single was demolished when you woke up one day to the fat fact of thirty-two and alone. Kashif was two years older, clean-shaven, with precise, even features: sharp eyes hooded intelligently into his face, and a small nose perched over the patrician bud of his mouth. He was an immigration attorney in Manhattan, he'd told her, where he worked on deportation defense and asylum claims.

In the weeks following, when they began seeing each other, Kashif spoke more and more of his aversion to Lahore—the swarming relatives and unhappy marriages, the conservatism, the filthy air. His father was a politician; his mother bustled like one. They were both powerful landowners in Punjab. Farah loved the idea of Kashif: a man determined to live via a rule book he'd assembled with care, neither his parents' son nor a cologne-drenched drifter.

"In my relationship with my mother," Kashif told Farah, "I can either be a prince or a courtier. I'd rather be a pleb in Manhattan."

That was more than a year before.

So much had changed.

She was in a stinky rural town in Pakistan, and this was her life. She slipped the hip flask from under her thigh and tipped it into her mouth: the bracing rush of gin and cucumber. Sweat slid between her breasts. September brought with it the illusion of respite, but it was always as muggy, as rotten, as July.

The dog resumed its staccato bark. Farah pinned a mosquito to her wrist and flicked it away. Her *kameez,* soft with sweat, clung to her back. What would her life in New York have looked like? She'd imagined a media office on the twenty-fifth floor of a sun-tinted building. She'd pictured herself in a low-cut blouse in a bar, atop a swiveling chair, leaning into Kashif.

She lit another cigarette and watched as the flame from the lighter flared in the crimped white gleam of humidity.

"There she is," said Kashif, walking up to Farah. He ruffled her hair. "Hi, beautiful."

She smoked her cigarette as she squinted at the darting light in the fountain.

"You know who desperately needs to get shit-faced?" said Farah. "Your mother."

Kashif snickered.

"God, what I would give to see that face crying tears of love and humility."

Kashif looked at his shoes. He smiled ruefully. "It's so weird. I honestly sometimes forget that the elected representative is, in fact, Abba."

"It's so obvious who wears the pants," scoffed Farah. She looked up. "She wouldn't be so insufferable if she were a *little* nice. A *little* aware of the words that come out of her mouth. I've decided I'm going to tweak my approach to her."

"To what?"

"To something more effective than rolling over and playing dead." She got up and crushed the cigarette under her *khussa*. "As discussed, two more days and we're out of here. And the Internet is shitty. What's the point of being rich if you can't have decent Internet?"

"Two more days, babe."

"I know you think my job is whatever." She took a sip from the flask. "But it's important to me." She swiped a drop of gin from her mouth. "I'm doing all the commissioning. Ambreen fucked off to Toronto after her wedding. On top of that—this weird village and your weird-as-fuck family." She screwed the cap on the flask and dropped it into her cloth bag. The alcohol loafing in her veins acknowledged her feelings with a bright bleak ease.

"I have immense respect for you. And your job," said Kashif as Farah walked away. "I'm the one currently without a job."

"You'll be fine," Farah laughed, looking up at the stars. "Turns ouuuuut you're more prince than pleb."


Next morning ZB, Farah, Kashif, and Saleem *mamoun*—who'd hurtled from Lahore in his open-cabin Vigo after a phone call from his older sister—assembled, before lunch, in the garden. They were sitting on checkered green-and-white folding chairs on a sheet of soggy green. The branches of ZB's pomegranate trees crackled in the wind, the leathery skin of the fruit swirling yellow to light pink to red.

The Willoughbys had departed after a tour of ZB's projects— the women's embroidery unit, the community kitchen, the girls' school—and ZB seemed very pleased with how it had all gone off.

Saleem *mamoun* was a compact man of fifty-five, mustached and pink, in the way of ZB's family. To compensate for his height, Saleem *mamoun* wore subtly heeled leather brogues.

*"Appa,"* said Saleem *mamoun* to ZB. "What did the Willoughbys say about the community kitchen? Gutted to have missed them."

"Well," said ZB, gravely. "They were most impressed. By the cleanliness. The menu for the poor. One's *hard work*."

"Excellent," said Saleem *mamoun*. "Did they agree to sponsor the water filtration plant?"

"No." She retrieved a mandarin-and-mint hand cream from her purse. "But they will." With difficulty she pushed back her bracelet-watch; the gold links had dug into her flesh.

Saleem *mamoun* examined his cigar. "On my way here," he said, and puffed on the cigar's fading embers, "the police stopped my car for speeding. 'Going to Begum Zareena Bokhari's,' my driver said. And they stepped away! Saluted me!" His left foot stirred in a triple tap on the grass, of what Farah sensed was a kind of spooked hollow humor at his own lifelong inadequacy, and a slow-burning distress, as he sucked on his cigar and his eyebrows crouched over his eyes, at the burgeoning influence of his sister. "Most impressive," he whispered.

"ZB's a heavyweight now," said Farah with sunny exertion. "She's more powerful, more loved, than the actual office-holder."

"Hundred percent correct assessment," said Saleem *mamoun*. And he sat up. "This wife of yours . . ." He looked at Kashif and cocked his head from left to right with a teasing glint in his eye. "Better watch out! Heh heh!"

Farah ignored Saleem *mamoun*. She said, "The people of Maujpur look to her to solve their problems. I've seen it with my own eyes. She's an innate problem solver. A born leader, in other words."

"Agreed," said Saleem *mamoun.*

"But optics matter," said Farah, getting up from her chair. "And on that front, I'm sorry to say, Maujpur leaves a lot to be desired."

"How do you mean? Can you give me an example?" asked ZB, who'd been listening silently, and now spoke with cursory benevolence.

"Mansoor garlanded Cynthia Willoughby with half the cash he put around Jon. Remember? And why? Because she's a woman, so she's half his worth. That's the first thing I noticed. I'm sure she noticed it too. They work in this country. They're not idiots." She laid her hands on Kashif's shoulders.

"It's just a silly garland!" panted ZB. "God! The priorities I tell you!" She looked around at the trees and sky and hedges, as if summoning her witnesses. "And Mansoor doesn't know any better."

"You should tell him," said Farah. "So it doesn't happen again. It's stupidly retrograde. You don't want your donors to think you're feudal—which, of course, we all know you're . . . not."

"Why doesn't someone else oversee trivialities like these?" hissed ZB. "One has too much on one's plate. One is up to here"—a slicing gesture at her neck—"with all the work."

"I can," said Farah, calmly. "Seems I'll have to."

"By all means," said ZB.

Farah kneaded a stubborn muscle on Kashif's neck.

"Ouch, dude!"

"Just relax," said Farah.

"Excellent advice," said Saleem *mamoun,* drawing on his cigar in the shimmering heat of the September morning. "Everyone should just relax."

Later that night, as Farah and Kashif lay on the hard high wooden bed in their room, Farah hugged her husband. He was brainy. He had a stocked bar. He was not on Twitter.

Kashif curled up behind her, pressing his body along her curve, the fronts of his feet touching the backs of hers. Farah remembered the first time she'd smelled his hair and neck and was able to understand—having been for days awed by the global sheen of him—all that was in Kashif, and herself, in the lives they had lived unknowingly apart.

Through the faded chintz curtains a scorched breeze gusted into the room.

"You know I love you, right?" she said.

"Yep."

⁓

NEXT MORNING, Farah and Kashif woke up late, at 9:00. Farah had missed breakfast with ZB—a ritual dear to her mother-in-law—but she'd resolved not to live in fear. Besides, Saleem *mamoun* would've kept ZB company at the dining table: a bit of quiet time between the siblings to vet the village gossip and soothe one another's lingering grievances against the world.

But ZB and Saleem *mamoun* had gone out, Farah was told upon entering the dining room: ZB to the site of the community kitchen, Saleem *mamoun* in search of partridge.

The dining table was vacant, its white cloth smooth and creamy in the morning light. Through the bolted windows, dust-choked sun poured into the room.

Kashif devoured a four-egg omelet studded with green chili. Farah sipped tea. Glancing at her phone she saw three messages from her boss: a video; a message saying, "Man standing at periphery—Kashif's uncle, correct?" and the third, stamped ten minutes later: "confirm, please." She clicked on the video. A girl, a teenager of about fourteen, was being paraded naked on a street, urged forward by a man wielding a stick. A circle of men surrounded her. Her hands were strewn over her face, and she was wailing, begging for someone to rescue her. The video showed Saleem *mamoun* at the edge of the road. He wore sunglasses, and lowered them every few seconds to observe the ruckus. He continued standing on the periphery, arms folded stoutly across his chest. The teenager shrank with shame as she was marched on. After a while Saleem *mamoun* detached himself from the crowd. The video continued for a few seconds as onlookers clustered around the girl.

A pit opened up in Farah's heart. "Kashif," she said. "Oh God."

"What happened?"

She passed him the phone.

"What the fuck is going on?" said Kashif, holding the phone in his palm.

"The poor child is obviously being made to avenge somebody's honor. For something or other. But what is Saleem doing just standing there?"

"What the fuck is he doing just *watching*?"

When ZB returned to the *haveli* at noon, Kashif and Farah followed her to her bedroom. They locked the door and drew the curtains.

"What's he doing just *standing* there?" said Farah. "He should have immediately intervened to help the girl."

"Calm down, Farah," said ZB. Her eyes remained fixed on the video. "Stupid, stupid, Saleem. And to make matters worse I hear the Chief Minister is on his way. He loves getting into his helicopter these days!"

"Saleem *mamoun*'s phone is off," said Kashif.

"He's gone hunting for partridge," said ZB.

"We heard," said Farah.

There was a knock on the door. Kashif opened it, and Mansoor walked in, his feet bare. It was nothing to worry about, he reported: it was just a family feud. The girl being paraded—well, her brother had eloped with a young woman from another clan. The offended clan was demanding blood. A compromise had been reached that the absconding youth's *sister* would be marched naked through the street to avenge the shamed family's honor. It was nothing to worry about, Mansoor said, for the matter was between two small families. The Chief Minister was indeed on his way, but he was going to the paraded girl's home, for a photo op. The matter would die down within hours, Mansoor said, as ZB could very well grasp. The girl was back in her parents' home, recovering, eating well. Her father had apologized to the Chief Minister for his actions. Everything, Mansoor offered with a thinning smile, was under control.

ZB thanked Mansoor and asked him to take his leave. Farah looked at her phone to see a message from one of her colleagues at *The Daily Imroze*. He was filing a report, he said: he would have to mention that Syed Saleem Qureshi, the brother-in-law of MNA Syed Mahmood Mauj Darya Bokhari, had been seen at the site of the incident. The reporter added he would've omitted the name of Kashif's uncle had a video not surfaced.

"Can you ask him to remove Saleem's name?" said ZB.

Farah shook her head. "There's visual evidence."

"He's probably going to be named in the police report," said Kashif. "He was a bystander to the violence."

"What violence?" said ZB.

"A girl being marched naked through the streets," said Farah. "That kind."

"I can get Saleem's name removed from the report," ZB muttered encouragingly to herself. "The local officer has frankly been waiting to do me a favor." She rose from her bed. "Now is the time."

"Absolutely not," said Farah.

"You will do nothing of the sort," added Kashif.

"You know what the people of Maujpur will say? 'If she lacks the power to prevent her brother from being named in a police report, how will she and her husband help us?' It's very well for you to offer your opinions. Your father has to win elections."

"This is not about Abba," said Kashif. "Stop trying to protect your brother."

"You haven't a clue about how things work here. Elections aren't won by being a saint. You have to deliver for your constituents, come hell or high water."

"That's hilarious," said Kashif. "You're exactly like the rest of them. That's *pathetic*." He made for the door. "And since when have *you* become the de facto MNA?"

"One has to protect oneself. To live to fight another day. One has vastly improved the lives of the poor."

"There's a difference," said Kashif, his hand on the brass

doorknob, "between freeing them from poverty and making them dependent on the whims of your kindness."

"I have provided employment opportunities to no less than five hundred women," said ZB.

"And in turn bought their devotion and silence," grunted Kashif.

"Stop it, both of you," snapped Farah. "This is *not* about the two of you." And she asked ZB, firmly, to send for Saleem *mamoun*.


Hands in checkered Burberry-raincoat pockets, Saleem *mamoun* mounted a stuttering defense: he was on his way to Salampur, having passed the cotton farm, when his driver pointed to the crowd and stopped the car. *He* had done nothing, he exclaimed.

"That's precisely the point, Saleem *mamoun,*" said Kashif. "You should have intervened. Called the police! You did *nothing!*"

They were back in the garden, Kashif and *Saleem mamoun* pacing on the grass.

"Do you know how ridiculous you look standing there?" said ZB. "For God's sake, you should have called *me*." She was sitting on a folding chair, a *chaadar* wound ominously around her mouth in a vague primal gesture of solidarity with her husband's constituents, whom she could not, as this very moment, reassure of her vast, overreaching powers.

"As we speak," she said, "the Chief Minister is at the girl's house. Scoring points!"

"The three of us should go," said Farah. "To make sure the girl isn't harmed in the coming days. The Chief Minister will leave in thirty minutes. The news will move on."

"What about me?" asked Saleem *mamoun* in a low voice. He scratched his earlobe.

"You sit tight," said ZB. "And keep your mouth shut. And don't leave the house for God's sake. Kashif, please stay with Saleem. Someone should stay with him."

ZB wanted to take two of her security guards along. Farah refused, saying they would go modestly. The overture was not a public relations jaunt, Farah added. ZB could so easily make the story about her: Farah knew this, and ZB knew, too.

To Farah's surprise, ZB did not argue.

"He's stupid, Saleem is stupid," said ZB, climbing into the passenger seat of the Prado. "But he's not a bad person."

"All he needed to do was to alert someone," said Farah, starting up the engine. "You. Me. The police. Someone better equipped to handle the situation. But he stood there quivering in his designer sunglasses."

"Sometimes one gets caught in a crowd. No? Important to remember that he neither provoked nor participated in the act."

"Yes," said Farah. "He stood there like an idiot while a girl was marched naked in front of him." She clamped her free hand on the wheel. "Everyone has a phone. Nothing goes undocumented. You know better than anyone how much anger there is against people like you. I'm just amazed at Saleem *mamoun*— watching the whole thing like it was a fabulous parade."

"What if they take him to jail?" ZB clutched the handle as her body heaved to the left. Farah drove silently over the potholes on the gravelly road. She'd been trying to place every argument in the towering scaffold of ZB's self-interest. The SUV churned clouds of dust, clods of earth. Stones flew by the tires. Green-yellow fields of double-crop rice swayed on the sides of the road.

Farah had not sought to learn about Maujpur, but the more time she spent with her in-laws, the more the land seemed to give off its secrets, its remote rhythms.

When they arrived on the outskirts of the town, thirty minutes later, Farah checked her phone for the news: the Chief Minister had departed for Lahore in his helicopter.

Farah parked the car three streets from the house. ZB and Farah placed *chaadars* on their heads, tucking the cloth behind the ears with only the eyes open to view.

A glinting stream of sewage water ran in front of the homes along the street. Pink and blue and white bags of torn plastic skimmed the sludge. A knot of mosquitoes huddled atop a floating blue water-bottle cap. The entrance to the house was a white cloth tied to the doorframe. Farah pulled the cloth to the side as ZB passed through, hopping over the gray slush. They walked into a concrete courtyard open to the sky and vacant but for a *charpai* and two large steel cauldrons, upturned, in the corner.

A toddler in red underwear, his eyes lined with kohl, scampered out of a room. A woman followed him.

"Who's in the house?" ZB asked the woman.

The woman tipped her head in the direction of the room. "The girl? She's in there."

Farah knocked on a painted white door. She heard a shushing sound.

"Who is it?" asked a man's voice.

"Syeda Zareena Bokhari," said ZB.

The door was hastily unbolted. A man of about ZB's age touched his hand to his forehead. He slid to the side.

A sunflower-printed velvet blanket covered a low-lying single bed.

In the corner of the room the girl sat with her legs drawn to her chin. Farah recognized her from her hands, the fingers long, elegant, tanned. "What's her name?" asked Farah.

"Rukhsana," said her father.

He pointed to the woman stroking Rukhsana's arm. "And she's her mother."

As Farah lowered herself to sit beside Rukhsana, the father said, "Rukhsana is a very good girl. She is a very brave girl."

Farah asked Rukhsana how she was feeling.

"She's much better," said her mother, placing a hand on Rukhsana's head.

"If anyone tries to harm you, I'm going to string them upside down," said ZB. She stood in the center of the room. "Don't you worry, my child. I will not let anything happen to you. I'm so sorry for what you had to endure."

"The Chief Minister was here," said the father, smiling bashfully. "He has sent the police after her brother. And he has accepted my apology. He knew I had no choice. What a humble man."

"The smarminess won't work with me," said ZB, her voice cutting. "If anything happens to this child, I'm going to hold you accountable." Her eyes burned. "Do I make myself clear?"

"She's my child," he said, looking at Farah. "Would I do anything to her?"

"You felt no compunction marching your child naked through the streets," said Farah.

"They wanted to kill her, but we made a good deal—"

"Hush!" said ZB. "Not another word."

In the presence of everyone Farah asked Rukhsana if she wanted to stay with her parents.

Rukhsana said she wanted to die.

Her eyes were a terrifying void.

Farah put her arm around Rukhsana's shoulder. "Your safety and security is the most important thing," she said, her voice breaking. "Everything will be fine. This is my promise to you. You have my word. Your brother will have to repent, and go to jail for making you suffer for his sins."

"As soon as we locate him," said Rukhsana's father, "I will drag him here to prostrate himself before your feet."

"Oh, but that won't be enough," said ZB. "How *dare* you humiliate the poor child like this. Did you think I wouldn't hear of it? Did you think I would sit back and watch? Unlike the Chief Minister, I actually care about the welfare of women."

"I'm going to see if there's a place for her in Lahore," Farah said to ZB, worried that Rukhsana was at risk of suicide. "She can stay with me for a bit."

"Correct," said ZB. "Good."

"What's your favorite food?" Farah asked Rukhsana.

Rukhsana was staring at the floor.

Farah placed her hand on Rukhsana's and told her she would return the next morning.

The father wanted to escort ZB outside, but she stood like a tower in his way. "If anything happens to this child," she said through gritted teeth, "if she gets so much as a scratch, the police will know whom to look for." She clasped her hands and said calmly: "And of course there is nothing worse than the wrath of a Syeda."

He averted his eyes and crossed his arms over his chest.

In the car, ZB was quiet—puffy jeweled fingers around the handle, face to the fields. The balancing act of subtle terror and sudden kindness; the gaudy command of local sensibility; the concealment of the self to make room, ceaselessly, for the personality: these were the facts of ZB's life, but she seemed to not know, much less want, a more authentic life.

They drove on a reddish dirt road in the dusty, sun-faded air.

"I'm worried she might drink insecticide," said Farah. "Important to get her out of here as soon as possible."

"Correct," said ZB, looking out of the window.

"Didn't Mansoor's first wife ingest rat poison?"

"Did she?"

"You told me!"

"Oh."

"So disturbing. It's becoming a trend among the women."

"Oh dear."

Farah sighed, she slammed her foot on the accelerator.

As ZB lurched forward, gripping the handle, she turned to Farah and said: "Exactly right—how right you are."

They returned to Maujpur in a deepening twilight. In the distance, from a patch on the still, flat horizon, flames rose to the sky. Smoke twisted across the fields. A scrappy Ferris wheel twinkled dangerously on a stretch of empty land. Farah turned in to the road leading to the *haveli*. A long-abandoned car, now a snarl of metal and grass, lay at its edge. Sachets of Head & Shoulders fluttered from a roadside kiosk. A string of fairy lights crisscrossed the front of a boxy house. Perhaps a boy had been born.

As Farah drove up the ascent, Mansoor stood by the *shisham* door talking rapidly into his cellphone. The *haveli* was dark but for its lit, sand-colored alcoves.

Mansoor slipped his phone into his front pocket and dashed to open the car door.

"All well?" asked ZB.

"By the grace of Allah," smiled Mansoor.

The door of the *haveli* opened, and its iron chain thumped. Kashif stepped out, his hairline matted with sweat.

Kashif leaned in to embrace his mother. Mansoor edged to the side.

"They took Saleem *mamoun*. Let's discuss. But inside."

"Who took him?" said ZB, pulling away.

"The police, Ma."

"And what did you do?"

"It was the right thing to do."

"Why didn't you call me? You should have called me immediately."

"Inside, please."

"He'll be here tomorrow is my guess," said Farah. "I wouldn't panic."

From the dining table in the reception room, Farah pulled out a chair for ZB. She slumped into it. Her shoulders, shrouded in wrinkled floral cotton, drooped.

"What did the police say?" asked ZB helplessly, looking up at Kashif.

"They want to ask him a few questions," said Kashif. "Why he was there, what he observed, why he didn't alert anyone."

"My own brother being marched into a police station! The TV channels will have a field day with this. Just imagine the stuff they'll say. Your father will be so embarrassed."

"Poor Abba. Poor you. So embarrassed and so powerless."

"I'm sick of your condescending attitude." ZB whacked her fist on the oak tabletop. "You're *not* the one running for reelection."

"And neither are *you,*" growled Kashif. "Stop pretending like

this is your cross to bear. If Abba cares so much about this constituency, he should spend time here. Rather than using you as a
front. If you're going to act like the local bloody chieftain, why
don't you run for a seat yourself?"

"The women in our family don't run for election."

"They're control freaks who run everyone else's lives instead.
How true."

"At least your father's doing something with his life. For his
own people."

"Leaving New York to look after you was the real mistake I
made. Knew it then. Know it all too well now."

ZB looked up, her eyes moist.

"Kashif," said Farah. "We made contact with the girl. I have
a plan. Let's all calm down."

"If I live to see tomorrow," said ZB, rubbing her ribs.

"What of it?" said Kashif. "You've lived to see today. What
good has it done?"

"A rich person is like a bird in the rain," said ZB, looking
away. "When it shakes off its excess moisture, it fills the thirsty
reservoirs. One must help those less fortunate."

"The girl needs your principled support," said Farah. "Not
your excess . . . wateriness."

And ZB furrowed her brow at the table's impenetrable glaze
of dark oak.


On the hard high wooden bed, Kashif curled on his side, his fist
clenched.

Farah covered her legs with a white sheet.

She turned on her side.

A moment later a hand flopped by her waist.

"I want to go back," he said.

"We'll be out of here in less than twenty-four hours."

"I don't mean Lahore, I mean out of this shitty country. I made a mistake."

"You're angry right now. You'll be fine tomorrow."

"You're so calm!"

"Families are families."

"She's getting on my nerves."

"Only natural: she's your mother."

"No wonder my sisters fled. She's a bully. If she cares so much about this place, how about giving power to the people? But no! She wants to sit atop the rot!"

"It takes time to institutionalize things. She's not so bad."

"Nor very maternal."

"The residents of Maujpur would disagree."

A whistling breath bounced from Kashif's nose.

She squeezed his hand.

She sat up on the bed. She slipped on her brown moccasins.

"Where are you going?"

She wrapped a *chaadar* around her shoulders. "Be right back."

Kashif turned dramatically on his side.

Walking through the first courtyard, Farah closed her eyes and inhaled the night-blooming jasmine.

# A Man for His Time

The rot on the dry bed of the canal sizzled: shards of broken glass, whiskering seeds of mango, boxes of fruit juice flattened and crusted with mud. Hafeez squatted by the pavement and scrunched his *kameez* in his lap to keep it from touching the ground. A cricket match was under way inside the empty canal. A boy in his late teens stood at the wicket—a small wooden chair—his lower lip tucked behind his teeth. As the bowler swung his arm into the air, a police officer trundled in from the road waving a wooden baton. He smacked the bowler on his back and the boys scampered away, grabbing the chair as they went. Hafeez stood up and shook out his *kameez*. It had been only six months ago that Hafeez, at a friend's urging, had entered the spotless new ablution fountains at the mouth of the university mosque. He bowed and knelt on the mats in the large prayer chamber inside, and later sat in the shaded light of the courtyard with a group of students. He rubbed his heels into the marble floor, the cool sharpening his senses, reminding him of simple pleasures. Had it not been for the Islamic Students'

Ittehad, Hafeez's days would have slipped by in the blankness of waking, wandering, hitting balls.

It was unusual for a university mosque to be made with marble but the administration had grasped the churning on campus: Jamil Khan had popularized a course on Islamic history and, through it, kindled a spirit of activism. It was said of Professor Jamil's classes that though he'd not asked his students, the women had begun sitting on the right side of the classroom, the men on the left, exquisitely separate.

Hafeez had not had the opportunity to take a class with Professor Jamil: seats vanished the moment registration opened up. It was something he planned to do before he graduated.

～

SITTING AT A TABLE in the university cafeteria, cocooned by the shouting joviality of his best friends, Hafeez bit into the last of his egg-and-*shami-kabab* burger, and the charred, most delicious bit of the burger bun slid down his throat. Just a few days ago he'd been made the secretary general of the Islamic Students' Ittehad.

Omar *bhai,* the president of the group, fiddled with a pack of cigarettes. An ancient white ceiling fan pushed around the stale, thick air.

Hafeez scraped his chair closer to the table as Omar *bhai* tipped his chin into the cluster of six boys. He was stouter and shorter than Hafeez, but his corpulence had its own rosy splendor.

"The liberal brigade is becoming clever," said Omar *bhai.* He looked up, at no one in particular. "A complaint has been lodged against us. Eh? Restoring modesty on campus is now called 'bullying'!"

The Islamic Students' Ittehad had circulated flyers on campus discouraging female students from wearing jeans.

When a student tweeted a derisive response, Omar *bhai* arranged for the student to be ambushed and, very lightly, seized by the collar. The student was reminded he was in the minority: surely he understood the implications of being outnumbered. And he was let go.

The student tweeted once more that he'd been threatened by the boys in the Students' Ittehad. Omar *bhai* denied any such ruckus.

Mopping *kabab* crumbs from his mouth with the coarse pink tissue wrapped around a bottle of Pepsi, Hafeez thought of his own secret cowardice. He disliked encountering physical violence. The neurons in his brain fired with distress. He was happy to meet his opponent in a debating arena, but he couldn't bring himself to slap or tug or punch. One day the Students' Ittehad would need Hafeez, his scholarly touch—even his impeccable fearfulness.

Besides, beating dirtied his *shalwar kameez* and made him sweat.

Over the deafening chatter in the cafeteria Omar *bhai* cleared his throat: "If you see something for the next week, just let it be. Do not react. We don't want to be trending for the wrong reasons." He looked at Hafeez and said, "They will all come around eventually."

He scraped his chair back, straightened his *kameez,* and walked out, ashing his cigarette on the sticky gray floor.

As Hafeez walked out of the university gates, Lahore revived to an early-evening clamor: crows gashed black against the sky, horses drawing carts skittish on the roads. Hafeez loved how the *azaan* rose above the blare of car horns and the call of birds gathering at dusk. It was a mesh of sound that evoked Lahore at its most stark, its most beautiful.

Though Hafeez could now afford to take a rickshaw home, he chose to walk. He was saving up for his sister's wedding: Kiran, suddenly so grown-up, to be married at nineteen to their first cousin Waqas, who worked as a car mechanic down the alley where Hafeez and his family lived.

As Hafeez stepped through the door of his home, he could still hear the murmur of conversing minarets. He took off his leather sandals at the door, washed his face and hands and elbows, and prayed on his maroon-and-white velvet mat in the swelter of his room. He prayed for his mother's health, for his own, for money: as much as Allah could spare. Hafeez glanced through the door to the kitchen, where his mother stood, a *roti* pinched between her fingers over a naked flame. The skin around her fingernails had thickened from years of exposure to stove fire. His mother had made up for her husband's incompetence by doing odd jobs in the city until Hafeez and his brother were old enough to contribute funds. She'd worked as a sweeper for the government; she'd worked as a maid in a rich home; she'd sat cross-legged behind a sewing machine at a tailor shop where the ceiling in the loft had been so low that she'd seemed like a toy in a gruesome dollhouse. Still, stitching clothes had been less embarrassing than mopping public bathrooms. Hafeez remembered the smoky, clotted reek of urine. He recalled the unlit, dank cubicles that his mother had scrubbed crouched on her legs, a worn wet cloth in her hand that she doused in a red bucket and swept on the concrete floor. She would shift the weight on her feet, a swaying trudge on her haunches, urging herself forward in thick rubber slippers. With her bare fingers she placed naphthalene balls in latrine holes from which rose hot fumes of shit.

Beyond the kitchen, Hafeez's father, Billa, was lying on a *charpai*, his fingers laced over his stomach, snoring. The snore climbed to a nasal pitch until it sputtered, tripped over itself. It thinned to an exhaling hiss. Hafeez watched his father's stomach as it rose and fell, and he felt repulsion. Diazepam to treat Billa's seizures, ZC 81 to quell anxiety, ZC 82 to help him sleep. Whether the seizures demanded the pills, or the pills had infinitely submerged his mind in a fog, it was hard now to discern. The pills had become, though, a technique to block out the demands of life. On occasion Hafeez had been forced to fetch the pills as Billa convulsed. After taking the diazepam, Billa would lie down, still as a corpse. After he'd taken 81 or 82, his jaw would slacken. Hafeez and his mother had counseled Billa to ease the dependence on medication, to go for a walk around the neighborhood. Billa had disappeared for three days when Hafeez tried to wrest the pills from him. Hafeez found his father outside Azeem Medical Store, slumped on the pavement.

Billa had collected plastic bottles and pieces of trashed iron to sell, until his epilepsy struck.

These days he slunk around the house, asking his wife for money, which she relinquished in carefully rationed amounts, in return asking him to not touch her.

Now the sight of his snoring father filled Hafeez with impatience. Billa had done nothing for his family, yet he acted like a decrepit king, fed and clothed by his wife's and children's money. The force of Hafeez's disgust had dented his ability to think clearly: he understood this about himself. He flung the newspaper with which he was fanning himself into the trash barrel. Billa had been laid off his job at a printing press when Hafeez was fifteen; he'd not sought another. How could Hafeez have mercy in his heart for a man who'd transferred, overnight, every burden to his wife?

He walked up to his mother in the kitchen and told her the house would be better off without Billa.

"Are you mad?" she said, smacking a *roti* on the *tawa*. "People will say his own family threw him out! Have some shame. Now get me a glass of water."

❧

OVER COOKED CHAI in the cafeteria the next day, Omar *bhai* reminded Hafeez and the other members of the Students' Ittehad about a protest on Mall Road. A young girl from the town Maujpur had been marched naked through the streets, and a women's NGO in Lahore was organizing a rally to protest the deed.

The steel table wobbled, spilling Hafeez's chai into the chipped saucer.

"These women have a bigger agenda," said Omar *bhai*. "They want parliament to change the words 'honor killing' to 'murder.' You get me? The secular brigade is trying to change the concept of protecting one's honor altogether."

"Everyone knows whose payroll they're on," said one of the boys.

"These are the classic antics of the anti-Islam brigade," said Hafeez, wiping the spilled tea with a tissue.

"Exactly," said Omar *bhai*.

"Basically," said Hafeez, "these people are following the Western agenda of secularism under the banner of 'women's empowerment.' This is the new global system."

"Total fact," said Omar *bhai.* "Well done." He leaned back in his chair, placing his baby-like hands behind his head as his eyes met Hafeez's. "I'll meet you boys at the march. I want to show you something."

On Mall Road a row of *peepals* created a canopy of green. The trees grew dense into the sky, and where the black branches jutted out, their broken shadows mingled with the green of the leaves. Patches of light leapt, twinkled, fell apart. Hafeez had lived in Lahore all his life but he relished anew his first glimpse of Mall Road every time he turned onto the tree-lined thoroughfare. To Hafeez's right, a marble pavilion held a bronze model of the Quran where, many years ago, a statue of a stuffy British queen had stood. If only Professor Jamil would run for public office, he thought suddenly, and he smiled.

He was amazed at the paltry turnout: some four hundred people clustered around a moving van. A billboard with the words *Lahore in Bloom*—cartoonishly painted flower bouquets—formed the backdrop of the moving procession. A man with a plastic tag around his neck brought a beige megaphone under the mouth of a severe-looking female activist. Her sneakered feet, dotted with mud, were splayed in a mannish V. Her face contorted briefly as she drew a deep breath and gripped the megaphone in her fist. "I would like to thank all of you for coming. From the bottom of my heart I salute your compassion, your courage, but most of all your humanity. Violence in the name of honor is unacceptable."

*"Unacceptable!"* the voices came back.

Hafeez joined the march from the sidewalk: he had arrived promptly at Omar *bhai*'s request.

The workers of the Communist Kissan Party waved red

hammer-and-sickle flags, breaking away every now and then from the main crowd to jump, shout, and scream in a circle composed exclusively of their party members. Hafeez wondered, as he had so often in the past, why the communists loved wearing tight jeans. The Che Guevara T-shirts he understood, but why reduce one's gravitas by wearing feminine jeans?

He saw a group of fifty or so women marching ahead in a drove. Their arms hoisted a banner of red ink on white cloth: *There is no "honor" in violence.*

The march stopped briefly, and the activist with the splayed feet climbed onto a sluggishly moving truck. She raised her arm, fingers outstretched, and a man pulled her up. The man's expression was one of grim importance as he stood behind her, concealing her body as best as he could: humidity and sweat had squashed her *kameez* between her buttocks. A crew of reporters—cameras jammed onto their shoulders—ducked in and out of the protesters' faces to zoom in on the woman's.

Standing at the top of the truck, the activist raised a hand in the air: "Friends, comrades, brothers and sisters."

Hafeez saw three police officers monitoring the protest. Omar *bhai* stood at the edge of the road. He smiled at Hafeez.

"As you all know," said the activist, "a young girl was recently marched naked through a town in Punjab to compensate for a transgression committed by her brother." Her voice rippled through the megaphone. "Violence that wears the garb of honor is an *affront* to the religion of the Prophet. These barbarians are bringing a bad name to our religion, is it not? It is time, friends and comrades, to put an end to these medieval practices. Our women will *not* suffer for the crimes committed by their husbands or brothers or lovers. We will *not* stand by in silence."

Her speech meandered into a sermon on women's rights, but she became, toward the end, gravely poetic. "We shall see," she said, invoking the verse of an old progressive poet. "Indeed we shall see the promised new dawn."

A member of the Communist Kissan Party howled in solidarity, and the procession lurched abruptly forward.

People shuffled onward in two broken lines, confused as to who was leading the march—the women or the communists?—but committed, it seemed, to a vague idea of something.

Then, a canister of tear gas hissed along the fringes of the pavement. The women lifted their *dupattas* to their eyes; they began to shriek. They charged toward the police officers in a drove, and the officers confronted them with riot shields. Another canister skirted the edge of the road right where Hafeez stood. An acrid smell crammed the air. Hafeez's eyes burned. He ran forward, then he ran backward. Tears tore down his face. He was coughing, he seemed to be choking. The women screamed, and a contingent of lady police materialized to ward them off.

Hafeez saw Omar *bhai* standing by a car in the far distance, a mask on his face. He waved to Hafeez. Hafeez reeled toward him, a river tearing down his face.

In the car Hafeez gasped for air; he could barely breathe. Omar *bhai* presented him with a water bottle to flush his eyes. Hafeez emptied the bottle over his face, and Omar *bhai* handed him another one.

There would be articles in the newspapers, he told Hafeez, against the violent tactics of the government. "So simple, so smooth." He smiled. "The government should know we are their natural allies, not these women. I organized the gas. But the government will bear the brunt of the anger for a law and order situation. They *deserve* it for not supporting our agenda," said Omar *bhai*, his eyes sharp. He looked at Hafeez with renewed expectation, his lips set in a small pout, anticipating, from his junior, a statement, question, or declaration he could seize upon. Hafeez only nodded—his eyes and throat burned—as he looked at Omar *bhai*'s jowly face. He squeezed the water off his nose. Omar *bhai* had hinted at a surprise, but Hafeez hadn't anticipated tear gas. He wished Omar *bhai* had told him in advance. Often, even the senior group members didn't know what Omar *bhai* had planned until the scene unfolded any which way before them.

From where had Omar *bhai* obtained the gas?

Hafeez sneezed into his elbow and looked away.

The ride back to his house was quiet. The sun hung low in a sky streaked with pink. Omar *bhai* gazed out of the window, his face reddened with happiness. The car bumped along Mall Road, passing first a traffic light, then the Governor's House.

It was only as the car stopped outside the alley of Hafeez's home, and he got out, that he asked Omar *bhai* where he had procured the tear gas.

"By dishing out money. Notes. Thousands of rupees. Nothing comes for free."

"Of course," said Hafeez. "May Allah protect you," he said, and shut the door of the car.

In the veranda Kiran paced beside a wall, sniffling into her *dupatta*.

"What happened?" asked Hafeez, touching his sister's hand.

Her shoulders shuddered.

"Tell me," said Hafeez. "Sister to brother. Heart to heart."

"What heart to heart?" The kohl in her eyes had smeared, shedding black flakes on her cheek.

"*Ohho,*" said Hafeez. "Just spit it out."

She told him she thought Waqas no longer wanted to be with her; that, of late, whenever she'd called him he had rebuffed her, made excuses. "He even told me," she said, "that this *rishta* was done against his will."

"Nonsense," said Hafeez. "The two of you were promised to each other at birth."

"Then why is he acting crazy?"

"Boys are stupid. He doesn't mean it." Hafeez smoothed out his *kameez*. "Everything will be fine. Waqas is an emotional type. I thought something serious had happened." And he sprinted to the bathroom to douse himself with water.

Omar *bhai* had asked Hafeez to write up what he called "the ideology" of their group. He was in the process of setting up a website on which he would display Hafeez's summary of their mission statement. Hafeez was the intellectual among them, Omar *bhai* had reminded him. It was true that four days a week, after class ended, Hafeez tutored students in English and Islamic studies. He charged a fair amount but it was his only source of income, some of which paid for his father's medication.

In a clean *shalwar kameez* Hafeez sat cross-legged on the floor of his room and, chewing on the top of his pen, wrote the opening paragraphs of their mission statement, in which he emphasized "veracity, justice, and Muslim dignity" as "supreme" virtues.

In his history class Hafeez learned how the word "Lahore" came to be. It was a boring lecture given by a woman with thick limbs and a splash of purple running through her short gray hair. She was the only female faculty member who didn't cover her head. The purple streak in her hair, the diabolic mood and gumption of it, was a provocation, Hafeez knew.

"Hindu legend has it," she said, surveying the room, "that nearly three millennia ago, Loh, one of the sons of the god Rama, hero-king of the Ramayana, founded a city on the banks of the river Ravi. Do you know what he called that city?"

Hafeez stared at her inked hair. Her breasts slumped.

"He called the city '*Loh-Awar*'—'The Fort of Loh' in Sanskrit."

Somebody snickered from the back of the classroom. "Fort of Loh or Fort of Lun?"

The students laughed nasally.

"I'm glad evoking the male appendage gives you so much joy. One more word and all of you, I repeat, *all of you* will be marched to the Vice Chancellor." Her jaw was tight, her lips buttoned. Hafeez would never understand her groveling accommodation of other people's cultures and beliefs. "Indians and Pakistanis have been, for centuries, the same people," she would plead in ten different ways. He wanted her, just once, to exalt Islam without finding a way of cheering on the Hindus next door. Her suspicion of her own religion was why the country had become schizophrenic, fissured between those who aped the West, reaping handsome rewards in dollars—like the women at the march—and those who, like Professor Jamil Khan, understood that strength lay in unity.

The professor picked up a book, held it close to her face, and began reading in her declaiming voice. "Situated on a plain at the opening between the mountains of Kashmir and waters of the Indus"—she looked up—"Loh could not have chosen a more scenic location for his city. Today, we know *Loh-Awar* by one of the modifications of its name that survived: Lahore."

The bell rang and Hafeez slid his books into his backpack. He whispered in his friend's ear. "Fat bitch, can't stand her."

"I wouldn't fuck her if you paid me."

"What about in Indian rupees?" cooed Hafeez.

"Dollars, baby, dollars!"

"HAHA! *Bhenchod!*"

Hafeez took care to avoid the coils of fresh horse dung on the road outside the university. The scent of fried food and fumes churned in the air. A shirtless vendor plunged a flour-coated potato into a scalding vat of oil and fished it out on a scrap of newspaper, on which, bizarrely enough, was a photo of Hafeez's favorite actress: Mehak Ahmed. Hafeez chuckled. His *kameez* flapped behind him in the breeze; twigs and candy wrappers crackled under his sandals. A drop of rain fell on the piece of newspaper, and he looked up at a sky tufted with gunmetal cloud. He wished it would thunder. Lahore was never as magical as when it rained.

He turned in to a long, deserted alley and saw, in the distance, his cousin Waqas sitting on a low boundary wall next to an older-looking man. The older man held Waqas's hand in his lap; Hafeez watched as the man guided Waqas's hand slowly, under his *kameez*. Hafeez stopped walking; he hid behind a wall. He gripped his cellphone. He suddenly wasn't so sure if he should divulge to Omar *bhai* the whole picture of what he saw, or thought he did: if he told Omar *bhai* he'd seen Waqas touching another man, Omar *bhai* was deranged enough to beat Waqas to a pulp.

On the phone Omar *bhai* asked the exact nature of the problem. "I need you here," Hafeez said, watching as the older man finished up, secured his drawstring, and hopped off the wall.

By the time Omar *bhai* and his two companions emerged from a rickshaw, Waqas was sitting alone on the ledge, talking dejectedly into his cellphone.

Hafeez told the boys he'd seen Waqas strolling through the alley holding hands with a girl—this, just weeks before his wedding to Hafeez's sister.

The four boys walked over to Waqas with the subdued menace of a gang.

"What have you been up to lately?" Omar *bhai* asked Waqas.

"Sir, *salaam*!" said Waqas, hopping off the wall.

"No need to *salaam* me," said Omar *bhai*.

He slapped Waqas.

Waqas stepped back, dumbstruck.

"This man right here, whose sister you're going to marry, he is a brother to me. Do you know what that means?"

"I'm not sure what you're talking about. He's my cousin."

"Oh, I'm very sure you know what I'm talking about." In a pounce Omar *bhai* seized Waqas's head and slammed it against the wall.

"What the fuck do you think you're doing?" screamed Waqas, cradling his head as he slipped to the ground, kicking up a cloud of dust.

"I should be asking you that. No?"

"Keep your fucking hands off me," said Waqas.

The two boys gripped Waqas's wrists and pinned them to the wall as Omar *bhai,* standing above him, kicked Waqas three times in the gut. "GET YOUR HANDS OFF ME," cried Waqas, his body writhing against the wall.

Hafeez crouched on the ground and punched Waqas errati-
cally on the lips. Waqas let out a terrified yelp. Hafeez glanced
at his own knuckles, white where the blood had left them. "I'll
take it from here," Hafeez said, his heart thudding. "It is after
all a family matter."

The boys let go of Waqas's hands, and Waqas shielded his
face as if shutting out a harsh sun.

He spat on the ground: a spray of blood soured in the dust.

∽

WHEN HAFEEZ ARRIVED HOME, he announced to his mother
that Kiran was not to marry Waqas. When his mother asked
why, he said, "Because I've said so." He took off his watch and
placed it beside him on the *charpai*.

"I understand," she said, sitting down on the *charpai*. "But
this is very sudden. You must tell me why you're saying this."

"Isn't it enough that I'm saying it?"

"You're my lionheart. My prince." She laid a hand on his
shoulder. "But she's also my daughter."

"Would I want something bad for her? Who else can you
rely on?"

"I'm not doubting your intentions. But I need an explanation.
You can't call off her wedding because you feel like it." She got
up from the *charpai*. "And my firstborn, by the Grace of Allah,
sends me enough from Dubai to keep this house going."

"Why don't you move to Dubai with him?"

"Why are you acting mental?"

"Why are you doubting my intentions?"

"How can you just call off her wedding?"

"Why should I provide an explanation? You should have
faith in me."

"That Omar is a bad influence on you," she said, tossing a hand in the air. "Don't think I haven't noticed how you've changed since you joined that Islamic group."

"It's true: I pray at least four times a day. Can you say the same for yourself?"

She smiled. "Foolish boy. I'll talk to you when you've calmed down."

Hafeez flung his arm over his eyes. The pain on the sides of his forehead always came on suddenly, and the June heat didn't help. The migraines caused him distress: he worried he might have inherited his father's epilepsy. With thumb and forefinger he pressed on his temples to keep the pain from bobbing up. He could easily have told his mother the truth about Waqas. But she'd picked a fight with him. He who loved her. He who thought constantly of her welfare.

Kiran's friends slipped in and out of the house, always saying *salaam* but rarely making eye contact with Hafeez. They'd begun preparing for the wedding to be held at the end of the month, and Hafeez's mother hummed along, occasionally garlanding Kiran's friends with roses and being showered in turn with petals. Specks of silver sparkled around her eyebrows. Billa slunk around the house in a shadow. He didn't notice the reserve between Hafeez and his mother. Neither Hafeez nor his mother communicated what had transpired between them. It hurt Hafeez to stifle his ache—his mother was the only person in his life whose strength and sunniness warmed his heart—but she'd settled, stubbornly, on opposing him.

Two days after his confrontation with Waqas, Hafeez's cellphone rang as he sat clipping his nails in the veranda.

"*Salaam,*" said Hafeez.

"*Wa'a-laikum-as-sal-aam!*" said Omar *bhai,* with operatic bounce, as if his utterance would win him a recitation award. He complimented Hafeez on his excellent write-up of the ideology of the Islamic Students' Ittehad; he said the ideology had been particularly effective on Facebook—shared by more than a thousand people. Their next step, said Omar *bhai,* was to write a short note advising students to make videos from their cellphones of professors who preached secular ideas in the classroom. "Easiest way to spot the troublemakers, of which there are only a handful left!" He told Hafeez an influential TV anchor would help them circulate the message. "All right," said Hafeez, throwing his nail clippings over the wall and into the alley outside.

Hafeez heard a shuffling noise at the door. Waqas walked in, his lower lip scabbed. He prostrated himself at Hafeez's feet, begged Hafeez to hear him through. He told Hafeez he'd been forced to oblige the older man—a retired professor who had first approached Waqas on campus. He'd seen Waqas sitting on a bench with a girl in the Science Block; he had told Waqas he'd get him expelled. It was so easy, he'd said: he'd spread a rumor that Waqas had disrespected the Prophet of Islam—the accusation would spread like wildfire, and Waqas would have no means of protecting himself against a crowd that in a matter of seconds became a killing machine. Unless Waqas did the professor a favor. What Hafeez had seen was the enactment of the awful favor. Waqas clasped Hafeez's hand: Could Hafeez not imagine the nature of the situation?

"Kiran complained about you before the 'situation' arose," snapped Hafeez. "What was that about, you fucking faggot?"

"Couples fight. We had a fight. I hung up on her. Then we made up. Please don't call me that."

"I don't believe you," said Hafeez.

"I'm willing to swear on the Quran."

"I don't want your filthy hands anywhere near the holy book."

"Just believe me. I beg of you. He threatened me and I was scared for my life."

"Just get out," said Hafeez. "Right now. Before I have to call my friends again."

"At least hear me out."

"I'm saying it calmly this time: get out of my house."

"As you say," said Waqas. "But I'm telling you the truth."

As soon as he left Hafeez slipped on his sandals. He plucked a tuberose petal from a bouquet wilting inside a plastic vase in the veranda and sniffed it sullenly. It was the rich man's flower, but how happy the poor were to decorate their weddings with it!

Hafeez knew not to invite Omar *bhai* into his confusion. Perhaps there was someone else he could consult. He knew who it would be.

A rectangular sheet of steel pasted on the wooden door displayed the words *Jamil Khan*. Below, a taped piece of paper with the professor's office hours. Hafeez had arrived a fraction late. He ran a hand through his hair. He knocked.

"Come in?"

"*Assalamalaikum,* sir."

Professor Jamil looked up over his glasses. He was much younger up close, his eyes radiant, his brown hair combed into a middle parting. "Office hours are over," he said, scribbling on his notepad.

"I'm not in any of your seminars, sir," Hafeez said. "I've come for a personal reason. I just need two minutes, sir."

Professor Jamil squinted. He put aside his notepad and crossed his legs. He looked at the clock on the wall. "You have my undivided attention for exactly two minutes."

Hafeez narrated, as clearly as he could, the incident he had observed in the alley. He said he had not told anyone because he feared for Waqas's life. "But I punched him in the face, sir," said Hafeez. "I got some friends in the Students' Ittehad to beat him up. By the end of it he was crying. Now he has fully apologized."

"So you used the Students' Ittehad to settle a personal issue?" said Professor Jamil. "Not very smart if you ask me. Family matters should always be settled behind closed doors."

"I thought you would be proud, sir."

"What does your father say?"

"He doesn't know, sir. Sorry, sir."

"No need to apologize to me." He tapped his pen on the writing pad. "Now, if you'll excuse me." His eyes flicked to the clock on the wall. "As you can see, it's time to pray."

In the curling damp and steam of a June afternoon Billa lay on his bed, arms slack by his sides. A scrap of light from the window danced on his gaunt leg. "I need to discuss something with you," said Hafeez, shutting the door of Billa's room. "Can you sit up for two minutes?" Hafeez looked at his father's face; his mouth was open and a thin drool of spit had curled by his neck. "O father of mine," said Hafeez. "I need two minutes, just two minutes, of your precious time." He came forward and shook Billa's legs. The left leg dropped to the side. Hafeez laid his hand on Billa's chest: silence where there should have been the uneven thump of a diseased heart. Hafeez looked at his father's face. It was loose, luminous, jaundiced. He covered it with the sheet at Billa's feet and walked out of the room. Hafeez went to the bathroom, lowered the plastic lid of the toilet seat, and sat down on it. He remembered when they had only a squatting toilet in the house. Hafeez had installed a flush toilet on which everyone in the family sat with comfort and pride. He got up and washed his hands. He wiped his hands with a towel, and stood, for several minutes, in silence, staring at the cold cement walls. He found his mother in the kitchen, retrieving a box of juice from the fridge. Hafeez laid a hand on her shoulder and told her Billa was dead. She put the juice box down, gripped his hand. She adjusted the *dupatta* on her head with a look of mild energy, as if settling, within her, several disputing emotions. She closed her eyes and muttered a prayer.

❧

BILLA'S SHRIVELED BODY is a white shroud in an open coffin. Rows of women have massed cross-legged before a heap of date palm seeds. They clutch the seeds—a kernel for every prayer— rocking, muttering, confounding the pain in ritual. Numbers and bodies matter today. Hafeez walks around; he welcomes the soundless embrace of strangers. It is okay to cry, though he has not. His father's body will be buried with the head toward Makkah. He has washed the body, bundled it, lifted it. A coherence infuses his ache. A friend sitting on the floor runs his hand over his dripping wet beard and acknowledges Hafeez with his eyes. The friend holds a chapter of the Quran in his hands. He is a scholar and will read for several hours: Hafeez needn't worry. Hafeez passes into the veranda. A light rain has begun to fall. People chatter, and their words, the quiet sipping of tea, the creaking of doors opening and slamming, breathe a mundane glow into the walls of his home. Hafeez watches as Waqas embraces his mother. He holds her firmly, his twiggy wrists around her back. She welcomes his clasp and brushes her face against his chest as she begins to cry. It is the first time in many years Hafeez has seen his mother cry. His heart pounds and he turns around and slips out of the veranda.

# *Tomboy*

He was the only boy I knew who didn't want to drive his own car. Muttering under his breath, he'd reverse it in a halting zigzag from the driveway, and as soon as we were on the road I'd slip into the driver's seat. We were sixteen when I bashed up the SUV his father bought him, my stoned face frozen in an uncomprehending smile as Zarrar Ejaz looked on in horror. He took the blame.

All those hours we spent playing *Street Fighter II*. I think of them now as a childish rehearsal for what our lives would become. Zarrar was always Chun-Li, a vixen in a puffy blue dress, forever flipping her legs in combat. I was Blanka, the wild green man from the jungle, likely to win but not without taking major hits.

After my father left us—I was sixteen, my sisters ten and eight—Mama began to lean on Zarrar's parents in a style they seemed to welcome. The rich like looking after the less rich so long as they look rich enough to blend in to their parties. Which Mama did, of course, offering herself up for every kind of service, from handmaid to boon companion to sounding board. Our mothers had been "best of friends" for three decades. Their whole cohort had carried over from school.

"Look at these two," Aunty Maleeha, the most lethal of the friends, used to say when Zarrar and I got in line to cut the cake at his overblown birthday parties. "The odd couple. You two should marry each other!"

"Say *InshaAllah*!" I bared my teeth.

Zarrar would scold me for fighting with Mama. "If I wax your mustache with my *own* hands you won't feel a thing," he pleaded. His curling fat hands reminded me of the mesh washing sponge in our kitchen but I didn't tell him this.

One day, before Zarrar could intervene, Mama bullied me into dyeing my upper lip blond with Jolen bleach. When I burned myself by wrecking the proportions of powder and bleach, Mama said it was because I showed no interest in "such things."

She was mother enough to splatter egg white over my mouth.

She struggled on her librarian's salary at the private school where my sisters and I were enrolled on a discounted fee. Papa had moved to Doha, where—we heard—he worked as an overseer on a large royal estate. Aunty Maleeha said, "Overseer means driver, manager, *what?*" Papa had been general manager at a nice hotel in Karachi; after the hotel shuttered he moved to Qatar, but he didn't take us with him. We learnt the bitter truth in bits and dribbles. There was a Malaysian involved, a woman he'd met at a shopping mall. "He didn't even think of his daughters," Mama said, casually smearing us with her grief while giving my anger the ignition it had always wanted.

A few weeks after Papa left Pakistan, our landlord stood in

his vest and *shalwar* at the base of the stairs below our Sea View apartment, a toothpick dangling from his pink mouth, and demanded advance rent. Mama's face sank into silence. "Some financial problems," I said, sliding down the stairs, though we had no financials and a ton of problems. Later that week Zarrar's father, Uncle Pervez, transferred money into Mama's account and told her it was what brothers did for their sisters.

Zarrar and my teenage years drifted in a haze of smoking hash in his bathroom, 7:00 a.m. breakfasts of *alloo channa,* late-night parties where I stayed sober so Zarrar could get drunk and I could drive him home.

Uncle Pervez worried about his son. Why doesn't Zarrar take an interest in sports? I would get asked. Why doesn't he have any male friends? What is this *obsession* with sketching Madonna? I assured Uncle Pervez that Zarrar was too smart for the girls he went to school with, that he would join his father's textile business when the time was right. I could blather like that with Uncle P. because we had a "good rapport," like the proverbial king and vizier, or some other faux-fraternal bond. It never occurred to me that he might be looking out for his own interests all the while grooming me to share his burden.

I tried to hide it, but the two years Zarrar was away in New York I was restless, empty. I had gotten used to being in his house, "hanging" with Aunty and Uncle like they were my own parents, driving Zarrar's SUV like it was my chariot, devouring the imported Boursin cheese from their fridge, tossing chunks of it into my mouth without toast, licking the silver foil clean. With Zarrar away, I began to drift. I smoked up during the day, was stoned at night in any case. I drove all over Karachi, inhaling it deep into my skull, sometimes driving far along Sea View, past the Village restaurant to a sandy nook overlooking the sea. Between the parking lot and the entry to the beach the view from my dilapidated sandstone wall was nice, and I smoked one, sometimes two joints, until I couldn't feel my dangling legs. Not talking about why Papa abandoned her ("Why are you asking *me?*" she would snap on occasion) was Mama's way of protecting us, but her anger bubbled over at the tiniest things—like when I threw out an empty bottle of hand soap without refilling it with water.

My friends at the Institute of Business Administration were easygoing, they were actually hilarious, we racked up a lot of jokes. They let me slip into their male world, a willing accomplice to every indiscretion, the cliquish slurs we had created for one another (*choot, cuntylaal*)—not like some of the girls, who were quick to express their delicate disgust. Still, I missed Zarrar and the way he defended my monochrome *kurtas* to Mama, the way he sat on my back when I asked for a massage. I wanted to hear about his magical life in New York—the clubs, the casinos, the bouncers, the booze. On the phone Zarrar said he missed me more than my stupid suspicious mind could comprehend, but when I asked him to tell me the *details* of his life, he said, *"I'll tell you when I'm home."*

Mama's friends suggested a few times that she remarry—the times are changing, they said—but Mama said she couldn't think of a thing more vulgar while she had three young, unmarried daughters sitting at home. I remember balking at that. Me? Get married?

Mama remained librarian at the school, but her evenings grew foggy with Lexotanil and the deafening yak of our TV. There were weeks where the TV just brayed at her ("Divorce??" "Marriage?" "Get out!") as Mama lay conked on the sofa.

"You need a man in the house," said Aunty Maleeha. "I have Asha," Mama said, conceding the void left by Papa to . . . me. I did the groceries, made sure the gas and electricity bills were paid on time, made sure my sisters kept their scholarships going. I even washed our landlord's car once a week while I hosed off our own Suzuki Swift, the engine of which kept stalling, but no one was ready to have a conversation about retiring the one "reliable" thing in our lives.

It made our landlord feel good that we knew our place.

In my second year at IBA Uncle Pervez offered me a job in human resources at his textile mill. He stood in his living room in his Bally slip-on mules, a hand in the pocket of his silk pajamas as two air conditioners as big as dolphins hummed above him.

He said independence was key. That I was an independent sort anyway. At sixty thousand rupees the salary was beyond my wildest expectation. I thanked him and he patted the side of my shoulder as if encouraging me to cheer up. I told him fifty thousand rupees would go into Mama's account and he said it was my money and I should do with it what I liked. "Now isn't that a wonderful thing?" He smiled, spreading his minty hands.

Mama said she was proud of me.

The same week Uncle Pervez called me into his office and told me he wanted me to give a tour of Karachi to a crew of documentary filmmakers from out of town. I was to show them the "hidden gems," the "local culture," the "underground scene." Too bad he left out "seedy underbelly," because two nights later Lucy Prest and I made out, drunk, at his house, in his son's bathroom under a poster of the Spice Girls.

The first time I saw Lucy she was standing by the bar in a plain white T-shirt tucked into a black knee-length farmer skirt. She was wearing brown ballet flats and a silver nose ring. No makeup. If you look closely, most women have restless eyes. Lucy's eyes were deadly, radiant, still. They were also blue. What can I say.

Lucy had managed to charm Zarrar's mother, a soft-spoken woman with ironclad boundaries. She had an arm around the hostess; she planted a kiss on the hostess's cheek, and Zarrar's mother shook with laughter like a dog shakes after a bath.

I drank as much as I wanted—no one to chaperone or drive home. Lucy and I snuck into Zarrar's bathroom and she let me touch her everywhere, moving my hand along her torso, along her thigh. Her legs were smooth, as if rubbed with light.

Lucy had come to Pakistan to make a documentary on the lives of workers who dismantled ships at the world's third largest shipbreaking yard.

When she wasn't filming I drove her around Karachi, taking her one night to my nook overlooking the sea. She hopped onto the sandstone wall and shared a joint with me though I could tell she didn't smoke. A masseur walked by shaking his oily glass bottles. I raised my hand to say *salaam* and he grinned so broadly I knew his life was falling apart. Lucy and I sat in the dark drinking beer from a brown paper bag. The field of air between her shoulder and my shoulder was electric and I looked at Lucy to see if she felt it but her arctic eyes were bloodshot.

She loved the *dhaaga kababs* at Waheed's. "Too much hygiene kills flavor, doesn't it?" she said as bits of *kabab* slithered from her mouth onto the plate. I thought she was adorable. For trying to impress me.

But a curiosity, an eagerness, an investigative thirst prowled within her. And few things irritate me more than people who ask too many questions too quickly. Before she left for England she grilled me on the phone about my "identity." I told her Pakistan was not Sweden. She said it would make me feel better to be honest about who I was.

"With all due respect, you don't know much about this place—or my family or my issues," I said on the phone.

"I know a little bit about—you?" she said in a British lilt that smuggled in opinions as dainty hesitations.

"That I look good in a leather jacket? And now you have a whole theory about me?"

"It upsets me to see you like this."

"You like seeing me half naked. I understand. Life is tough." She laughed. "I miss you."

"I miss you too."

"Do you think we're in love?" she asked.

"Hmmm . . ."

"Never mind," she said quickly.

"I'm just thinking . . ."

"If you have to *think* about it—the answer is no."

"I'm thinking about how beautiful your belly is, babe," I said, reprising a game Zarrar and I used to play, pressing it like a panic button.

"Will you visit me in Bristol?"

"I will," wondering how in the fucking world.

"You should ride a motorbike in Karachi. You'd look so hot? And change the whole culture around women riding bikes."

"Your opinion matters so much to me," I said, certain she'd miss the tone.

"Who were you talking to?" Mama asked the next morning as soon as I walked out of my room. I hadn't taken a piss all night.

It was typical of Mama to blurt without warning. It was her way of catching us off guard.

"Talking when?" I said, annoyed.

"On the phone. Last night. *I miss you too,*" she cooed. Then with a spurt of righteousness: *"babe."*

"Were you standing outside my room listening to my conversation?"

"Exactly—yes."

"Zarrar," I said. "I was talking to Zarrar." I don't know what went through my mind but I knew it was the right answer to give.

"Oh, *Zar-rar.*" She pressed down on the air with a clenched fist like someone who had lost a chance.

She had spotted one.

⌒

AND THEN ZARRAR RETURNED. With a diploma from Parsons. He hadn't bothered to do the four full years, just a two-year course his parents felt was more than enough. Lucy had departed for Bristol, not without telling me she thought I was a coward.

As I unpacked Zarrar's suitcase on the floor of his room, rummaging to locate my gifts—two pairs of identical black Diesel jeans, six white T-shirts, several packets of Wrigley's Big Red—Zarrar said, "Do you remember when Aunty Maleeha used to say we should marry each other?"

"Mmhmmmm . . ."

"Just checking . . ."

"How can I forget?" I yanked my jeans from the morass of his gunky stuff. "You know who else remembers? Uncle P."

"He's your boss now. So weird!" Zarrar laughed and sighed.

"Because he's smart," I said. "Because he knows."

⁓

I GOT MARRIED to clamp Mama into a golden—permanent—silence. "I have not one, not two, but three of you," she used to say, as if her daughters were benign tumors that had to be removed in order for her to be at peace.

Papa, we knew, had remarried. He sent Mama money for the first time, probably to assuage his tiny manly mound of guilt, what else. There were rumors he wanted to visit his ex-loved ones with his Malaysian bride.

Zarrar, meanwhile, was desperate to launch his own couture house, but he needed to be married first, to claim legitimacy in the eyes of his father. Uncle Pervez found the idea of a fashion-designer son distressing, and only a marriage, to a woman, could dump on it some dignity. Zarrar's mother was more advanced in her thinking: she knew her son was straight just as she knew night followed day, just as she knew that a dog in the house kept the angels away.

When I signed my *nikahnama*—at twenty-three—I glanced up at Mama's face, aflame with relief. Not a single tear was shed, such was the focus of her ambition. I wore a white *chickankari shalwar kameez* dotted with rings of silver metal embroidery. The shirt was tight under my armpits, but I appreciated, not for the first time, its bland, protective magic. Today was a day to shut up, to smile, to weep indebted tears.

Zarrar sat next to me in a white *boski shalwar kameez,* the fingers on one hand splayed over his thigh.

"Such a tomboy you used to be," tutted Aunty Maleeha, still

keen, after all these years, to demolish the barrier I had erected against her. "Look at you now, all married!" she gasped.

And I thought, yes, look at me now, getting on with my life, soothing my mother by stepping into the driver's seat once and for all.

⌒

A FEW WEEKS AFTER the wedding Uncle Pervez advises me to switch jobs. "You should be an equal partner in Zarrar's enterprise, manage the business side of things," he says. I want to laugh. The money flows from one source. His life's mission is to keep his son happy, fulfilled, in the arms of Asha.

I wonder how it's possible for father and son to be so different—Uncle Pervez a mindful little monster, his eyes never wavering from the prize, and his hapless son, who deals only in beauty and in comfort. Are they an equation, with one side furnishing the other and holding it in balance?

For the first six months, while Zarrar plans his debut collection, we outsource the dyeing, the stitching, the machine embroidery. Zarrar takes his sketches and fabrics to the tailors and dyers in the market next to Bilawal House. The tailors and dyers are young men as old as us. Their eyes never stray far from the sewing machines and bubbling blackened vats where the cloth is dipped, cooked, and fished out steaming with pigment. Zarrar hovers hawkeyed over a tailor as a switching pattern whirs into a velvet *choli* he'll never be able to wear in Pakistan.

"What would you do without me," I say, not posing it as a question, the fumy wind against my face.

After the wedding, Mama has morphed into a silent lighthouse. Occasionally she sounds a panicked drone of love and prayer—her love is inseparable from her fear—and I can't believe my luck at finally having her off my back.

Uncle Pervez calls every night to ask if "all is well," how things are "coming along" in our Clifton apartment, if the power supply and the water are "all set." It pains him to see the apartment unfurnished, he says; and then his wife grabs the phone and says she knows a very good interior decorator who does "solid stuff only" and she'll WhatsApp me the number right away.

~

IT'S COLD WHEN we drive up in our Jeep, the first of December, the wind strong, the sky clumped with black cloud. In the passenger seat Zarrar sits hunched over his phone. A calm has appeared on the faces of traffic wardens: Karachi may be experiencing a real winter . . .

The interior decorator's house in Lalazar has two gates. On the phone Nina Sheikh explains that the smaller gate is the entrance to her residence, and the larger, about twenty feet ahead, bearing the same address, is the entrance to her father's. We are told to come through the small gate.

We walk into a living room stacked with paintings: a still life of gnarled fruit; an abstract contortion of the naked body, red shading to orange; a family portrait in which four subjects look somberly away from one another. A small canvas shows a woman in a garden sprawled naked on a blanket. Her pubic hair is a black matte tangle.

A modern teak *jhoola* stands in the corner of the room. Terracotta figurines line the top shelf of a wooden glass cabinet. On each side of a white linen sofa are lamps with oblong white shades, their brass pipes visible through tubular glass.

"Welcome!" Nina kisses me on both cheeks. She smells of pepper and vanilla. She wears a purple sweater—the sleeves bunched to her elbows—black jeans, and a pair of dust gold bangles on one arm. She seems to be in her late thirties.

"You smell great!" I say.

"I make my own perfume," she says, shrugging and laughing.

"I'd love to learn," says Zarrar.

"Anytime, sweetie." Then with a dash of concern: "I hope the nudes aren't bothering you?"

"Why—would—they bother us?" we say together.

"It's your first time in my space. I don't want you to feel uncomfortable." She raises an eyebrow. "You never know who feels what these days."

Nina disappears down a long corridor and returns a moment later holding a silver tray, a bowl of chips, a bottle jammed into an ice bucket, three glasses.

"Almond sherbet," she says. "I don't believe in winter drinks or monsoon drinks or depression drinks. I say: drink everything and anything *anytime* and anywhere."

"Awesome," says Zarrar. "That's supernice of you." And I think, this is what a rich kid goes to America for: to distill the gentleman within . . .

She pours from the bottle and hands us a glass each. The almond sherbet is ice cold, hopping with scent.

"This is *in*-sanely good," I say, wiping my chin.

"The almonds are from Hunza. I'm glad you like it. So many congratulations, you two. It's always nice to see young people embarking on their journeys. I envy the idealism, I really do."

"You seem to have a pretty nice life," says Zarrar, gesturing to her living space.

"You're kind, *jaani*. It's my haven." She tosses her gaze to the walls and her eyes grow large as she grows modest.

"How's your father, Zarrar?" she asks.

"Busy, busy, busy—exactly how he likes it!"

"He was so talented," Nina says in a coiled whisper. "He's always been brainy. That was obvious from the very beginning. But I still have that sketch somewhere. Of me. Made by Pervez. He was *bhai*'s friend, as you know. His hand could move. Oh, his hand flew on the page!"

"He made a sketch of me when I was a baby," says Zarrar, a vehemence in his voice. "But never after that." He looks at Nina's paintings. His jaw is flexed.

"Happens to the best of us." Nina smiles. "I trained to be a fashion designer. Realized midway that I didn't want to decorate women for the pleasure of men." She fidgets with her dust gold bangle. "I hope that . . . doesn't offend you? I know you're a design—"

"Don't be so formal," says Zarrar. He gazes at her affectionately. "You're so polite. It's so unusual."

"Thank you. Shall we talk about your vision for your space?"

"We don't have a vision yet," I say.

"Minimalist with a splash of deco," says Zarrar.

Nina claps her hands. "A man who knows his mind!"

On the ride back home Zarrar is quiet. He looks out the window and says, "I like her."

"Me too," I say. "It's like she's from another world. First I thought she was kind of weird."

"Me too!" Zarrar laughs. "But she's cool."

"So different."

.

Zarrar decides he wants to present a collection at Fashion Week, which is only a month away. He doodles for a few days and comes back with an idea: Downtown New York meets Kalash Valley. Lots of reds, pinks, byzantine blues, canary yellows; cowrie shell and wool embroidery on jumpsuits, bomber jackets, *kaftaans,* sari pantsuits. I tell him I will model a bomber jacket for him and he tells me not to toy with his heart.

Nina is delivering a bed and a sofa in two weeks. We have a microwave and a fridge but we sleep on a mattress. She texts to say "good things take time" but we are her priority. She asks what we are doing on the weekend. "Not much," I text back. She invites us to her house for a get-together. "LOTS of interesting people. Promise you won't be disappointed."

Zarrar has a small crush on Nina. We go.

Nina's living room is dark and moody by candlelight. The paintings have mellowed in the gloom, but every now and then a flicker of candlelight on the walls casts a glow on the missing piece of a face, a wrist, a strip of gnarled fruit. Rose petals float in clay bowls. On a long glass table is a black marble cheese board with olives, grapes, cottage cheese, walnuts, and a sprig of thyme that I think is not meant to be eaten.

"Ahhh!" cries Nina, waving her hands, a cigarette pinched between her lips. She wears a tight wool dress, backless, one arm choked with steel bangles. She smells of pepper and vanilla.

"You look exquisite," Zarrar says matter-of-factly.

"I can't tell you how happy I am to see you both." She squeezes Zarrar's mushy bicep and tells him to get a drink.

So many familiar faces in the room—a twenty-five-year-old

stand-up comedian whom I've seen live, a queer filmmaker who delivers blockbusters on the lives of people very unlike him, an actress with big brown eyes whose name I can't remember, a Marxist professor in his sixties who has just been fired from his job at a college in Lahore for critiquing Pakistan's blasphemy laws.

Nina takes me by the hand into the huddle of a small group. "This is Asha. Asha, this is everyone. I'm too tipsy to do introductions." She pulls thirstily on her cigarette. "Friends, give Asha all the love because she's very special." She pushes out a cloud of smoke from the corner of her mouth. "Drink?" She elbows me in the ribs. "Is that even a question," I mumble.

"The thing with older men," the twenty-five-year-old comedian, Munizae Afreen, is saying, "is that nothing shocks them. They don't flinch when I fart during sex. Just *one* example." The Marxist professor laughs nervously, takes a long sip of his drink, then begins to chuckle wildly.

"I've found my next heroine, ladies and gentlemen!" The filmmaker raises Munizae's arm. "May I have your manager's number, please?"

Everyone laughs. The actress smiles with her eyes and slips away.

"But is Pakistan *ready* for a heroine like Munizae?" Nina interjects, slipping into the huddle and handing me a can of Murree beer.

"*Ooh*—you read my mind!" I say, cracking open the can.

"You're not hard to read, *jaani*."

"Pakistan is *faaacked*," says a new face. She seems drunk. She leans into Munizae and links arms with her.

"*Aa jao,* baby." Munizae makes room for her friend.

Nina says, "Asha's husband, Zarrar, is going to make waves in the fashion scene. Mark my words. I'm *never* wrong."

"You're so young," says Munizae, looking at me, tilting her head. "Only weirdos get married so young these days. Wait. Are you a weirdo?"

"Uh—Zarrar and I've been best friends since forever," I blurt.

"In this country," says Nina, "marriage gives women wings." She puts her arm around me. "That's just the sad reality. Look at the actresses—they get married to *halalofy* their careers. They literally get married so they can get on with the business of building lives and careers."

"And as soon as an actress becomes a superstar she drops her husband like a hot *paratha*," says Munizae. "Marriage *is* patriarchy; it's wild that I still have to explain this to people. First comes love . . . then comes rape?"

She flutters her eyes like a princess.

Her friend sniggers.

"Who wants a refill!" says Nina. She swivels around and jerks my arm, and we walk across the room. "Are you okay, *jaani*? Munizae is a live wire."

"I feel like I'm in another universe." I reach for the pre-rolled joint in my jacket.

Zarrar is talking to the model Ghazi Adamkhel.

"I just rescued your wife from a conversation that was about to go off the rails," says Nina with a gulping laugh.

Zarrar looks at me and I communicate with my eyes that I'm fine. I light up, my hand is slightly shaking.

"All okay?" asks Ghazi Adamkhel with the well-meaning stupidity of a stranger. He cups his tobacco goatee and leans forward, searching me for injury. Against the strain of his black

dress pants, his thighs bulge, curvaceous, on the verge of volup-
tuous, and for a moment, this detail, paired with his earnestness,
overrides my angst.

"All good, dude," I wink, and the smoke from my joint bil-
lows past his ear. He clears his throat and steps away like a
sergeant.

"What exactly happened?" asks Zarrar when we get into the car
at 1:00 a.m.

"Munizae—the stand-up comedian?—she was being a *choot*.
It's not like I'm *not* a feminist, but she's on a whole other level."

Zarrar reaches over and kisses my fist. "Did you have fun?"

"Nina's amazing. She knows how to manage people, which is
half the freaking job of living, no?" I rev up the engine. "What's
the scene with Ghazi Adamkhel?"

"He's getting married next month and he invited us to the
wedding."

"Ahan . . ."

"He's marrying his cousin."

"Ahan . . ."

"He told me his father sleeps with a Glock under his pillow."

"Ahan . . ."

"He looks like a Prada model." Zarrar sighs. "There's something so beautifully broken about his face."

I squeeze his hand and tell him he should invite Ghazi over.
The streets of Lalazar are quiet; from inside a home a bougain-
villea spills into the sickly glow of a lamppost. For a while we
drive in silence. The main road is deserted, but the wind is antic
and snappy, and it eddies through my shirt, bloats the brown
silk of Zarrar's. A blue water tanker trundles past us.

"Ya," says Zarrar blankly. "We should go see my parents on Sunday. Abba's really missing me."

"Do you really need me to come?"

"I thought you'd want to see them."

"Not really."

Zarrar turns his face to the window. "Up to you," he says.

⌒

"MUNIZAE AND HER FRIEND got smashed and crashed at mine. How are you?"

A text from Nina.

"I had a lot of fun," I type. "We should hang again."

"Whenever you want, *jaani*."

"Sunday??"

"Haha. Sure! I'd come to yours but you have no furniture . . . yet . . ."

"☺"

"Come around twoish?"

I spend the next day wondering what I should wear. I settle on jeans, a black sweatshirt, and *kohlapuri chappals*.

Sunday afternoon I drop Zarrar at his parents' and drive to Lalazar. He's in a bad mood, but he'll be fine after a dose of Uncle Pervez.

I drive up to the big gate, then remember Nina told us last time to come through the small one. I reverse quickly.

Nina's garden is plastered with fallen brown leaves.

She's sitting on her teak *jhoola* in a white *khaddar shalwar kameez* with a big scooped neck, yellow socks on her feet. The windows are open and the December sun twinkles on the glasswork on the *jhoola*. The paintings are flat and stark; they look tired after the party.

Nina gives me a long hug. "Inside or outside?"

"I want to try the *jhoola,*" I say, perching my ass on the swing.

"It's old," she says. "Doesn't really move."

"Very disappointing."

"Awww!"

I shrug cutely.

"Tea?" she asks.

"Beer?"

"Aha!" She disappears into the long corridor.

Inside the glass cabinet lined with terra-cotta figurines are framed photos: Nina's arms around the Marxist professor; Nina and Munizae at a Halloween party looking stormily into the camera, black teardrops under their eyes; Nina clutching a tiny dog. Nina as a child sitting cross-legged on a lawn, a spread of elders on folding chairs behind her.

"Here you go," she says, pressing a Murree can into my stomach.

"How do you know Professor Rashid?" I ask.

"He's my *chacha*. The only sensible one in the family. The only one who reads."

"This country has gone nuts. I feel so bad for him."

"Some Islamic students' organization mounted the campaign against him. But I don't get those people who think Pakistan's problems *begin* and *end* with Zia. It's like—no, sweetie. The nation-state is a problem. Majoritarian rule is a problem. Organized religion is a problem. A country whose only identity is not being the neighboring country is a problem. The invisibility of women is a *huge* problem."

"The women are very visible. Their lives are mysteriously hell . . ."

"I've low-key become an alcoholic," she laughs. "You know, I would love to choose—cherry-pick—my battles. For my own mental health. But you can't discuss women's issues without discussing 'culture.' But you can't discuss 'culture' because then they kill you."

"I used to worry about Qandeel," I say.

She fixes me with a look. The abject telepathy of shared despair.

I pivot to a lighter observation. "Munizae scandalized Professor Rashid for precisely one second until he realized everyone was laughing and he could also laugh *araam se*."

"Oh he *loved* it," says Nina, rolling her eyes. "He was saying how every single one of my friends is a game changer. I know Munizae is a handful, but she doesn't mean any harm."

"She's intimidating—but cool."

"You're also intimidating and cool, *jaani*."

"I can't tell if you're mocking me . . ."

"Why would I mock you? I think you're cool."

"Zarrar is cool."

"And so are you. Can I ask why you married him?"

"What do you mean?" My grip on the can tightens.

"It's a straightforward question."

"We're best friends."

"And?"

"We're best friends."

She drops it. She walks toward the *jhoola* and I follow her.

"You know the big gate a few feet ahead? My father lives there."

"I accidentally went there today."

"It's not a big deal. He's eighty-five. I'd made a name for myself when he gave me this place. Rented a room in a friend's apartment—*filthy* apartment—for a decade. Didn't speak to my parents for a whole decade. Was depressed, miserable, somehow never gave up on work. Worked like a maniac, actually. But I wanted to be honest about who I was. That was the one thing I was clear about. Now I have a nice house, it's true. One day, when I didn't need his help anymore, Abba called me over to tell me he was partitioning his house and leaving half of it to me. And, of course, my sister had already 'given' him three grand-children by then. And they'd given up on me by then. Now he's dying, he's like, okay, I don't want to die an asshole." She looks out the window at the fallen leaves. "Oh, I've forgiven them all."

I think of Mama and Papa and I want to tell her everything— maybe later.

"I know you and Zarrar care for one another," she says, sit-ting on the *jhoola*.

"He's a really nice person."

"I can tell you feel safe with him."

"Really? How?"

"That night at my place. You relaxed when you were with him."

She brushes the hair off my face. "This haircut suits you."

My face flushes red, flushes blue.

Nina says, "You know all the dark stuff in Munizae's comedy about her father's alcoholism and her parents' marriage? It's all true."

"Yeah. Very intense. I should get going, I have so much stuff to do at home," I say.

She kisses me on my nose. *"Dil hai chhota sa, chotti si Asha,"* she whispers.

In the Jeep, the tears are silent. I try to choke them back, old habit, but they're not having it. I flick them off my face as I drive out and beyond Lalazar, forgetting where I'm driving to.

Zarrar and I had gone to a party, we were fifteen, and as Zarrar stood in the line for the bathroom a bunch of boys pointed at him and called him "homo" and I just stood there.

When Zarrar walks in I'm standing by the window in our tenth-floor apartment ripping through my second joint. He hangs his leather satchel behind a chair.

"Forgotten all about your *majazi khuda?*"

I tell him Nina kissed me on the nose.

"OOOH! The lesbos of K-town crawling out of the woodwork! Love it!"

"Stop it, Zarrar."

He puts his arms around me.

I tell him I admire her guts. She's unlike anyone I've ever met.

"I told you from the beginning I thought she was cool," he says. He kisses my cheek. "Did you hook up??" he asks in a silvery breath.

"No."

"Why not?"

"We were talking."

"So nothing happened. That's adorable."

"Easy, Zarnish, easy."

A breeze topples from the sky. It snuffs out my joint. I fling it into the parking lot.

Zarrar pokes around in his satchel. "I have something better."

MDMA, everyone's new friend. I've done it once before with my college friends.

We each take a pinch of powder—I have no clue how much—and put it on our tongues.

Zarrar goes to the kitchen to get a jug of water.

I go to the bedroom in search of flip-flops.

In the cabinet under the bathroom sink I find a glow stick necklace.

I sit on the toilet and hold the glow stick in my hand.

There are many thoughts.

Eventually I fish out the flip-flops from under the mattress.

Zarrar is standing alone on the balcony, still as a statue. I pop the glow stick around his neck. He turns around and grips my shoulders. "Your eyes are very dilated." He hands me a glass of chilled water. I down the whole thing and place it on the ledge. Below, the asphalt moat glitters.

When I lift my head to the sky a gold moon twitches with light.

The palm tree to the left of the balcony is swishing in a slow dance, the fronds frothy, rustling with light.

"Everything's kind of on fire," I say.

I kiss Zarrar on his warm red ear.

"This tree is *so* sad." I point to the palm. "It's such a stunner."

Zarrar wraps his arms around me. He grins.

His tiny black speaker is playing house music, and I feel every scintilla of sound—of chimes and synthesized flute and even the whoosh of a passing thunderstorm—move through me. I look at my toes, pale and squat and dignified under a web of green night light.

A lightness drizzles over my face, my chest. As I grip Zarrar's hand my mind blazes with the certainty of my love for him. He has always protected me; I have tried to shield him.

"Everything's shiny, right," Zarrar says. "Feel very loose. Like I might blast off into space." He makes a sucking sound.

"Gorgeous stuff. Bloody hell."

A hammering light rings the moon.

He sighs. "Karachi can be pretty too."

"Karachi can be pretty too."

My hands dig deeper into my pockets.

My jaw is tight.

I blink away a shimmer in the corner of my eye.

The moon pulses blue-gold.

"Why are you crying, *meri jaan*?" asks Zarrar.

"She's brave," I say.

"Who is?"

# A Life of Its Own

## Part Two

They want to do a seat adjustment," said Mahmood. "A routine thing in politics." The newspaper crackled in his hands as he crossed one leg over the other, clearing his throat to lurch finally into the matter. "They want to give *you* a reserved seat, Zareena, my dear"—he lowered the paper—"provided I don't run from my district." He rustled the drooping edges. "A reserved seat is the way to go. Liaquat is a dirty player. He's bound to run a dangerous campaign. We'll save elections expenses *and*"—he turned to Kashif and blinked benevolently—"the emotional angst."

But ZB was looking at her son, who was gazing with a knotted brow at his phone.

"All okay, *beta*?"

"Farah's had a flat tire," said Kashif. "And she's all alone."

"Send someone to her at once."

"I offered but she says she's fine."

Typical, thought ZB.

She looked at her husband with incredulity. "Are you suggesting we let Liaquat have a free run? He'll continue oppressing the people. A reserved seat is a bribe, Mahmood. I don't want to be the recipient of a bribe. And I certainly won't bow and scrape before them. One is incapable."

"I'm seventy-six this year," said Mahmood. "I don't have it in me."

"Then find someone else to run," said ZB. "It's absurd to let that corrupt man go unopposed."

ZB turned to Kashif. "How's Farah?"

"Currently cranking the jack."

"Who's Jack?"

Kashif waved her away.

"We should find someone else to run," repeated ZB.

"How about you?" said Kashif. He looked up from the phone and smiled. "It feels more organic than Abba. You're the face of the welfare work."

"You want your mother to spend *lakhs* of rupees on a campaign?"

"It was okay when you wanted to do it?" said Kashif.

"Why can't she take the reserved seat and be done with it?"

"One, she's capable of annihilating Liaquat. Two, she doesn't want to sacrifice her *independence,* her freedom. Three, I don't understand why any of this needs to be spelled out to *you*."

"The tradition in our family—"

"The men in our family no longer make the rules." Kashif squeezed ZB's wrist. "You were born to do this. I know it. Everyone in Maujpur knows it. Now is the time. I'm telling you."

ZB's eyes welled up. She took a big, cold gulp of her tea.

Her children, and only her children, could move her to tears so wantonly. Her daughters had begun lives away from her; it was Kashif who'd abandoned a stellar legal career in New York to be with her after her heart attack. Of her children he was the most kind, upright, humorous. He bickered with her, held her to exceedingly high standards.

Her daughters had grasped their freedom over an absolute physical chasm. Zainab, her firstborn, had told ZB: "Being away from you allows me to love you." Nafeesa, her second-born, had vowed not to have children of her own. ZB was terrified of her daughters, and constantly wondered what she had done to repel them. They could crank from within her unknown reserves of guilt and fear. ZB had recently told Nafeesa, "The only person in the world who terrifies me is you." Nafeesa had snickered, in her eyes the withering look of a spoiled child.

ZB had been relieved when Kashif had introduced her to Farah. Despite occasional, trivial brawls with her daughter-in-law, she admired Farah, a sensible woman from a modest background who perceived more than she let on. Like Kashif, Farah was ironic and even-tempered. In Farah's case, the humor masked a sobriety that masked a deep and sensitive strength. Like ZB, who had unwound herself from the grip of her father's orthodoxy, Farah had waged a battle to do the things she wanted. She had been a scholarship girl and, later, gone to the best university in the country. At the age of twenty-eight she'd risen to op-ed editor at *The Daily Imroze*. ZB had never seen Farah as happy as in the days leading to her move to New York. Farah had brought out her suitcases, folded her one-piece swimsuit, poured silver-coated fennel into a ziplock bag. Then ZB had a heart attack, and Kashif changed his life around, moved to Pakistan. Though Farah had been disappointed, ZB never heard her complain.

Unlike ZB, Farah had married stupidly late (a thirty-three-year-old bride: an oxymoron!) It had given her a hard little eternal confidence; it had congealed Farah's preferences and dislikes into a state of mild neurosis. At twenty-three ZB had tripped into marriage; her late twenties had been a galling stumble into motherhood; her thirties and forties a season of erasure; her fifties quieter—the children had left home—as it was then, slowly, that she turned her attention to Mahmood's constituency.

As for her sixties, well, she hadn't anticipated they would be quite so *independent*.

Her husband was forever intrigued that ZB remembered the name of every man, woman, child, and elder with whom she came into briefly vivid contact. Mahmood never really noticed anything about other people—they were a scattering of eyes and ears in a self-replenishing social reality. ZB was charmed by his reluctance to linger on people's hidden agendas, but it was for this reason he'd needed her and her preordained gifts as a woman, to nurture, and to notify.

"Hi, sweetheart." Kashif embraced a sweaty, flushed Farah as she strode through the glazed red door of the dining room. She was wearing a white cotton *shalwar kameez* imprinted with stains of soot.

Farah rolled up her sleeves: "It's fucking boiling outside."

Of late Farah had taken to brandishing, ZB noted, colorful language in her mother-in-law's company.

*Fucking fools, fucking delicious, fucking elites.*

Farah had taken over the running of ZB's girls' school, from where she was returning. She had, much to ZB's irritation, made optional the *shalwar kameez* uniform for junior school. The girls could now choose to wear trousers and shirts. When ZB counseled that Maujpur was not quite ready for Farah's revolution, she had shot back: "Let's just respect the division of labor."

The only labor ZB was familiar with was the subservient kind.

But when ZB watched Kashif and Farah, her heart swelled with peace. Kashif was the child who had returned; of her three children Kashif was the balm of her old age. ZB's relationship with him survived on a blustery current of mutual respect. She adored him, knowing well he'd shunned a life in the public eye. He was too good for it.

"What would you like to eat, my dear?" ZB asked Farah. "I've had your favorite biryani—*without* the *aaloo bukhara*—made."

"Just water for now." Farah sat down at the table and retrieved a pack of cleansing towelettes from her purse.

"I can't drive, let alone replace a tire!" whooped ZB.

"I hear you're running?" asked Farah.

"One is talking about it."

"Don't want the reserved seat?"

"It's a fraud."

"Total fucking fraud," said Farah, dabbing her forehead. "But the thing is, female representation *is* contagious: seeing a woman in parliament encourages women to participate in the political process." She wiped her nose and scowled at the muck. "And, it turns out, women care about issues like water and health care, as opposed to men, who just want to build roads. Statues. Erections."

"Mahmood being the exception, of course," said ZB.

"The road leading to the *haveli* is literally named after him," scoffed Kashif. "It's cute when you invent stuff, Ma."

ZB twisted her mouth in an arch furtive O, like a schoolgirl.

Her husband smiled, rolled his newspaper, and exited the room.

"You should run," said Farah. "I'll help you. *We'll* help you." She held up the grimy towelette. "You *must* put air pollution on your agenda."

ZB reached over and patted Farah's hand. "My dear."

"Feel suddenly exhausted," sighed Farah, looking at Kashif.

"I would too if I were toiling in the heat for no clear reason," said ZB.

Farah smiled at Kashif.

She lay a hand on her belly.

ZB looked at Farah, then Kashif.

"I can guarantee your grandchild will be your biggest fan once you're elected," said Farah.

"Is this some kind of joke?" asked ZB.

"Why would we joke about something like this?" said Kashif.

"B-b-b-ecause Farah had always said she didn't want children so soon after marriage!"

"I'm not exactly a spring chicken."

"Oh, Farah! *Mera bacha!*" ZB's left hand squeezed Farah's, her right Kashif's. Her eyes glistened with sudden tears. "How wonderful. How wonderful. How wonderful. Is it a secret?"

"Just for now," said Farah.

"I must give *sadqa* immediately," said ZB, rising from her chair.

"Instead of slaughtering a black goat for thirty thousand rupees, how about presenting a check to the science lab?" said Farah.

"For God's sake, Farah, don't mock me," said ZB, gripping the corners of the dining table.

෴

TWO DAYS LATER ZB was sitting on a jute stool under a large banyan outside the *haveli* overseeing the medical camp she ran every Sunday.

She fanned herself with a splotchy plastic file. Some two hundred men, women, and children had clustered around the banyan.

The sun was sharp; so was the musty Maujpur breeze fluttering parched leaves, twigs, and the corner of ZB's *kameez*. The residents of Maujpur sat on chairs and *charpais,* their eyes following the two doctors in lab coats, stethoscopes dangling, making the rounds. It was here, in the open air outside ZB's *haveli,* that the people of Maujpur could avail themselves of the best diagnosis available to them for miles.

The medicines were heaped on a long steel table in the center of the camp. ZB could see that a dispensary would be her next challenge.

Dr. Ashfaq, goateed and bespectacled and about Kashif's age, leaned over and whispered into ZB's ear: "May I talk to you in private, ma'am?"

"What is it?"

"Best to talk privately, ma'am."

ZB stood up from her chair with the sedate good grace of a woman used to taking the long view. She looked at her swollen feet strapped in black Ecco sandals. Kashif had bought her a pair of sneakers, flashing his own pink pair, but ZB could not bring herself to wear big rubber blocks under her *shalwar*. She was traditional; she adhered to a type of feminine decorum. And she would always have Marks & Spencer on Marble Arch.

She walked the doctor across to the first and central courtyard of her *haveli*. The courtyard's floor-to-ceiling wall of blue and white tiles shimmered in the heat.

What Dr. Ashfaq told ZB didn't startle her: Gul Sanober, who ZB had seen skulking around the camp every week, who a month before had been diagnosed with the hepatitis C virus, was discovered to have been lying about her medicines. "Every week she comes and says, 'I've lost my medicines, can you give me more,'" said Dr. Ashfaq. "Four weeks she's done this, ma'am."

"Where are the medicines going? Haven't you asked?"

"This is the fourth week she's said she's lost them. I thought it best to bring it to your attention. She's here again today."

Dr. Ashfaq was asked to fetch Gul Sanober.

"Sit here," said ZB to Gul Sanober, pointing to the folding chair next to her. Gul Sanober sat on the edge of the chair, winding her limp red *dupatta* around her mouth. Gul Sanober's fierce beauty had somewhat retreated, ZB noted, her thick black plait was now parched and thin, her eyeballs tinged with yellow. She was in her mid-thirties, and a vine of wrinkles sprang around her lips.

"How are you feeling, Gul Sanober?" ZB asked.

"Please blow a healing prayer on me. I'm not getting better. I'm cursed. It's been months and months. I need a prayer from a Syeda like yourself." Gul Sanober smacked her palm to her forehead. She stared at the floor and let out an uncertain moan.

"You know very well I'm not in the business of blowing prayers. Tell me now, would you like to unburden yourself? I know how difficult everything is. I understand. You've been losing your medicines for three weeks. I'm just concerned. You can tell me, Gul Sanober. I promise I won't get angry. You have my word. I want you to get better, my child." ZB reached over and held Gul Sanober's skeletal fingers.

Gul Sanober said her husband had been selling the medicine she received from the camp on the black market. Every week, she said, he would force the medicine from her hand and instruct her to return to the camp.

"I thought as much," said ZB, sighing. "You must take the medicine here. No more bags to take home."

Gul Sanober said she could die and her husband wouldn't notice.

"You tell him I'm no longer providing it. Just put it on me. And if he bothers you, tell him to talk to me." ZB paused as she watched Gul Sanober's pale, haunted face contort with the threat of tears.

"Is your husband a drug addict, Gul Sanober?"

Gul Sanober burst into tears.

ZB embraced her. They rocked back and forth.

⁓

IN THE HOUR BETWEEN twilight and darkness, the streets of Maujpur took on a carnival mood. In the roadside shops, behind the glare of tube lights, television sets came scratchily to life. Teenage boys prowled on motorbikes, relishing the wind, their coiffed hairstyles, a sly adolescent aimlessness. Outside ZB's *haveli* the shrill rippling peal of a truck horn flared and died.

ZB folded her prayer mat. She had prayed for a healthy grandchild. She was determined to relive the joy of parenting—a much gentler model than her own. She wanted nothing more than for her children to see her for who she truly was.

The lights in the *haveli* had come on. She could hear stainless-steel lids clanging and sliding in the kitchen, the screen mesh door squeaking shut, Farah's voice straining over the discord of her staff. Mahmood's two sisters were coming to dinner and ZB's cook had prepared a big meal. As she bent down to strap her feet into a pair of soft gold leather sandals, she thought of how correct she'd been to consider herself a cut above Mahmood's sisters. In the early years of ZB's marriage her own imperiousness had alienated the sisters. The passing years had vindicated her. The sisters were all shawls and perfume and clucking suspicion.

Moments later Baji and Shaukat shuffled into the front door draped in black *chaadars*. Baji led with a walking stick; she complained of an ache in her back as she dawdled gradually in. Shaukat, the youngest, said the terrible heat could not deter her from meeting her only brother. Shaukat clasped Kashif's face in her fingers and squeezed it, savagely affectionate, left to right, right to left. Kashif, as ZB had expected, retreated to his room after saying hello to his aunts.

ZB hugged her sisters-in-law with sluggish, smiling ceremony. They moved slowly; it had been their habit, ever since ZB had known them, to make a gratuitous show of persecution. Shaukat embodied a brand of self-disfigurement particular to a rich woman in an unhappy marriage. The permissiveness of wealth—the bloated handbags, the sharpened emeralds, the smothered, diaphanous makeup—suggested a despairing aloneness. But it was none of her business, ZB reminded herself.

"It's good to see you, Baji," said Mahmood, steering his elder sister by the elbow into the drawing room.

As Baji lowered herself onto the cobalt-blue velvet armchair, Mahmood plucked the walking stick from her hand and placed it beside her on the lacquered wood armrest. "Bless you," said Baji.

Mahmood took his seat on the gold sofa facing his sister. "*So*. Kashif has suggested his mother run for a general seat in the coming elections."

ZB watched Baji's otherwise stately face twitch with distress. "But, Mahmood, it's *your* seat, and, Allah bless him, Abbaji's before that."

"The women in our family—" said Shaukat.

"Don't run for election," said Baji.

"Kashif thinks his mother should run."

"But surely, Mahmood, *you* should contest . . ."

"Not at this age, Baji. Anyway, they *have* offered Zareena a reserved seat for women in the forthcoming parliament."

"Well, then, that's settled," said Baji.

"What's the issue then?" squeaked Shaukat, fanning herself with her *dupatta*.

ZB could feel her irritation rising. Before she could interject, Mahmood revealed that ZB did not in fact *want* a reserved seat.

"It's like affirmative action, Mahmood," said ZB, using a term Kashif had brought to her attention. "Never mind," she whispered hotly, as she looked at the vacant, uncomprehending faces of her husband and sisters-in-law.

"Well, I mean I could consider it now that the kids are away," Shaukat piped up.

"You don't have a political bone in your body," said Mahmood with the swift, quashing honesty of a sibling.

"Didn't you say it was a *reserved* seat?" Shaukat rolled her eyes and wheezed a droll strangulated laugh.

ZB looked from one sister to the other. Nobody particularly noticed she was dumbstruck.

"So you want to *run*-run?" asked Baji, turning to ZB.

"I am seriously considering it," said ZB. "Especially after Kashif suggested."

"What does Kashif know?" sneered Baji. "This election business is not like the charity you do for the poor. It's war. Just take the reserved seat and be done with it. That's it." She mock-wiped her hands.

"We'll see," said ZB, looking at her golden shoes. "One has energy. Life is short. There is tremendous goodwill."

In the dining room, Baji spoke appreciatively of the cook, inherited from her and Mahmood's mother. ZB's dislike of Mahmood's sisters was in direct correlation to the effusiveness with which she served them: on the table were *nargisi koftay, pulao,* mutton chops, *haleem,* large *ghee*-flecked *rotis.* The more contemptuous she was of her sisters-in-law the more food she spun in her kitchen.

"There is nothing in the world like long-grain rice," said Baji. "Amma—Allah grant her peace in heaven—knew it had to be cooked in consommé to be perfect." ZB looked up from her plate of *haleem* at Baji's flushed, sagging face: none of the women was an independent entity. Everything flowed from the House of Maujpur. ZB's gaze traveled to the mottled green skylight and she thought of how, in the first decade of her marriage, Mahmood had begun spending the weekends in Maujpur to oversee his vast landholdings. She had wanted to accompany him—she was bursting with ideas about drip irrigation, digitizing the land records, creating women's work units. But she found herself in a bungalow in Lahore dashing from a six-year-old to a four-year-old. On occasion she'd slapped and spanked her children, a fact her foreign-educated daughters never failed to bring to her attention.

"What are you thinking, Zareena?" asked Shaukat. She stabbed a *kofta,* split it in half. "So quiet! Totally lost in thought! Feeling uspet about something?" she asked with the goading appetite of a woman who thrived on charging the banal with currents of apprehension.

ZB glared at Shaukat, who had four children—and not a single grandchild.

"Just counting my blessings," said ZB tartly. And she smoothed a crinkle on the starched cotton place mat before her.

❧

ON MONDAY MORNING ZB took a deep breath and pitched herself, her clean, unjeweled fingers grasping the door handle, into her open-cabin Toyota. If she was going to run for office, she would do it the right way. She had locked away her rings and earrings and embroidered *shalwar kameez*. She had replaced her grapefruit-scented Hermès *eau de parfum* with the fevered sweetness of a mere Body Shop.

As the Toyota swerved along the curving road of rough red sand, it blared away buffaloes and carts and motorcyclists. Kashif had dubbed this "the rural power drive." He wasn't half-wrong, ZB chuckled to herself.

Slowly ZB's tiny entourage swelled: village urchins latched onto the open back of the white Suzuki pickup truck trailing her Toyota. How fast information traveled these days, thought ZB, as she looked at the two teenage boys in the back of the Suzuki, flashing Vs with their fingers. Within half an hour, ZB had arrived at her farm, part of which housed a walled organic garden. Here she grew cabbage and radishes and carrots in the winter, and aubergine, okra, and bitter gourd in the summer. Three buffaloes provided full-fat milk, and she thought with a smile of the ready supply of organic milk for her first grandchild.

ZB's green parakeets squawked upon seeing her; a crowd of roosters and hens scattered as she walked toward the parakeets. Through the thin bars of the cage she fed them slices of raw guava and stood for a moment admiring them. They lolled their heads and glared back.

The two-acre walled garden, with its lime hedges, fig trees, and pungent young mangoes, in the middle of ZB's farm, was where she repaired to calm herself when her head felt as if it might burst with public pressure. The garden offered simple pleasures—lime leaves pressed into a sharp citrus fragrance in her palm; the bite of a ripe, silky guava; mangoes dipped in black salt that always put her teeth on edge.

In the middle of ZB's garden was a God-knows-how-old *peepal,* more ancient even than the banyan outside her *haveli.* She often retreated under the patchy green shade of the *peepal* to confer with her comrades. Today, in anticipation of her arrival, two wicker chairs, a low-lying steel table, and three pedestal fans with dusty cable leads attached to a faded wooden electrical box had been placed under the tree. A hundred folding chairs had been set out for her supporters.

The health workers, teachers, and volunteers who constituted ZB's network of organizers sat up as they saw her approach the tree. Abbas Daulah, spry and weathered in his white sarong, leapt to his feet, shuffling them into his silver-thread *khussas.* "Sond! Sond!" He waved to his fifteen-year-old son and assistant, who quickly switched on the mic. ZB raised her hand, she smiled. With her *dupatta* she patted sweat off her face as she took her place on one of the chairs facing a fan.

A mic was handed to the imam. A recitation from the Quran unspooled.

The mic passed back to Abbas Daulah, his wavy black hair grown to the base of the neck and swept up in a cotton turban. He adjusted his sarong with his left hand as he took the mic in his right.

"*Assalamalaikum,* brothers and sisters. We are gathered here today to convince Syeda Zareena Bibi that we want her to contest the forthcoming election as our candidate from the constituency. Now, everyone knows she doesn't *need* to contest these elections. Allah has endowed her with anything anyone could ask for: health, wealth, a handsome son. But we need her to step in. Take your turns, brothers and sisters, and convince her, for she owes this to us. Is she not our sister? Is she not our mother? If she won't liberate us from our oppressors—you know whom I am referring to!—why did she bother to build free schools, women's work units, and a community kitchen? Wasn't it so we could have our basic human rights? What, I ask you, is a greater human right than dignity? Doesn't Zareena Bibi know how our representatives, their land managers, the *police*—how they disrespect us? How they trample our hopes, our rights, our honor? We will restore our honor by electing Bibi. I welcome you all to speak your minds."

A long patter of applause broke out. ZB noted Gul Sanober's presence in the crowd. She was happy to see her, and she smiled warmly.

As ZB's well-wishers got up, one after the other, they spoke of individual stories of oppression, and relief through ZB's efforts and protection. Gul Sanober said she'd been frightened of ZB, but ZB had not judged her. Not only had she understood her plight, she had articulated a truth known only to Gul Sanober. Allah had blessed ZB with deep wisdom, she said. Safia, one of Abbas Daulah's two wives, snatched the mic from Gul Sanober midspeech. It was only here, in ZB's space, she said, that she was ever asked her opinion. If ZB had not had a stern word with Abbas Daulah, Safia would have been confined to the four walls of her home, shrouded from the world, she said. Safia looked pointedly at her husband, then at ZB. "For as long as Bibi lives," Safia said, "I know I am under her protection."

ZB felt the blood rushing, a peculiar knotted energy coursing through her limbs. She retrieved a cup of cooked tea from the table in front of her and took a cautious sip.

"You are a born leader," said Mansoor, the estate's manager. He stood up and straightened his *kameez*. "Allah is my witness. I have been telling everyone for twenty years that you are the real voice of the people. Mahmood *sahab* is a good man. A very polite and good human being, no doubt. But you are the *voice* of Maujpur." He paused, and added in English, "It is *fect*."

ZB smiled—she swatted a fattened fly on the edge of her teacup—and thanked Mansoor for his faith. She was a mere vessel, she murmured.

Among the whirring fans and air swirling with dust particles, a sober discussion began on ZB's chances against her opponent. She sat behind the steel table as several of her supporters stood up to make wandering, encouraging statements. It was said, by a tall man who introduced himself as a teacher, that though Liaquat was powerful and had the help of the state, ZB would probably win, for she had won the hearts of women like his daughter. She had worked selflessly, without gain or fame, for so many years. It was clear she was not doing this for the money. If there were a real opportunity to get rid of Liaquat, the women of Maujpur wanted to take it. ZB was listening carefully, noting the sincerity in his voice, as well as his disregard of electoral logic. Liaquat, said the man, had created a culture of fear. ZB was beloved, trusted, a mother—*their* mother.

"You and I are the same age!" ZB admonished from her chair. She wagged her hand. *"Leh!"*

A wave of laughter crested through the crowd. Gul Sanober dropped her *dupatta* from the clutches of her teeth and chortled with abandon.

ZB scrolled through the contacts in her phone book as Abbas Daulah reclaimed the mic.

*Ashfaq Khan Community Kitchen Cook; Bricklayer Baba Ata; Cynthia Willoughby Foundation; Dildar Shah Bus Driver; Farah; Firdous Carpenter; Kashif; Latif Qayoom Headmaster Aitchison College; MJ LATEST; MJ LONDON; Perveen Pest; Pest 2; Pest 3; Sajida Bibi Divorcee Teacher with Mole on Nose; Shah Muhammad Hussain Electrical; Shah Muhammad Hussain Hairy; Shaheen Ghulam Abbas Friend Made at Dunkin Donuts on Motorway.*

ZB looked up: she was being offered the mic. She put aside her phone and cleared her throat. "Thank you for your suggestions. I am humbled and moved." She drew a long breath. "The Almighty has been very kind. Very, very kind. Tomorrow, as you know, we inaugurate another water filtration plant. This is the third plant in our area and my dream is for Maujpur to have dozens of such plants." As hands came together in applause, ZB raised her own to quell the fervor. "But I want to create a culture of self-sufficiency. I don't want anyone to be dependent on the charity of the rich. We live in a modern age; we must act like we do. So I want to empower *you*. I want *you* to live with dignity. As you all know, one of the main causes of illness in our area is waterborne disease, and it breaks my heart to see so many children suffering. Children whose potential is limitless if raised healthy. *If* raised healthy." She spoke with an air of reverence and ache. "Now, the running of the plant will cost thirty thousand rupees every month. I would like you to know this will come from my own pocket." She shook her head bleakly. "There is no other option."

She took in the thundering applause.

This was how it was in politics: one could contradict oneself endlessly so long as one's audience grasped the things unsaid.

ZB set off for the *haveli* in the early evening, as the sun was shedding its splendor: ribbons of orange thawed into a lilac sky. She wound down the car window. The Toyota passed a patch of stubbly yellow grass on which a single cow, ribs jutting, grazed. The dry perished sweetness of a compost heap merged with the air. The scent was familiar, rancid, soothing. She closed her eyes to the warm breeze.

Her father had walked out of the labor room, subdued, upon hearing that his firstborn was a girl. The reaction was not unusual for a man of his time. And yet, the story had agitated ZB until it forged her.

She opened her eyes and sat up on the seat.

An extraordinary new chapter. A role she'd dreamed of longer than her children knew. She hoped, this time, she would not disappoint: she wondered whom her granddaughter would look like.

# Are You Enjoying?

Soni woke up to find Asher's sleeping face silhouetted against the marmalade glow of her table lamp.

It was 1:00 a.m., and Friday night had slipped into Saturday. "Fuck," said Soni. "Wake up. Wake *up!*"

She felt the first rousing slither of anxiety: always in the stomach. She had lived with it long enough to know its grip.

Soni's phone vibrated. Sarah's text: "Where are you?"

Asher looked at her with the drowsy, glutted smile of a lover. He was twenty years older than her twenty-seven.

"Don't give me that look," said Soni. "We need to move. *Right now.*" She peered at her phone. "I'm really sorry, Saroo," she typed. "Calling you in ONE MINUTE."

"You looked so nice in your sleep," said Asher, sitting up and buttoning his blue collared shirt. "Your mouth was closed and there was slight smile on your face. That's why I didn't disturb." He stood up and cleared his throat. "You should marry me."

Soni observed the twisty feeling in her stomach. She breathed carefully.

"I'm not going to be someone's second wife," she said, looking up from her sneakers.

"My religion allows."

Soni smiled and breathed.

"The man who marries you is going to be the most luckiest," said Asher. "When you get married I will look at you with same intensity. I don't have ego in that department. No matter what happens I'll always search for intensity in your eyes."

How to tell Asher she found his words odd, absurd, irresistible?

"You could be with anyone in world," he said. "But you've chosen me. I feel honored."

"I've grown up watching you." She rolled her eyes. "Waiters love you. Women love you."

He blushed.

"Listen," said Soni. "We have to limit our public interaction. People recognize you *everywhere* you go. Not good for my reputation."

"Yes, ma'am."

Outside, Soni's fort-like home glowed in the light of security cameras: red eyes that blinked within rotating black orbs.

In the frosty November air Soni flicked away Asher's hand as he tried to grasp her finger. "Can't you see the cameras," she said through gritted teeth. "The guards are watching." She exhaled sharply. "So nice to be stalked by machines in my own home."

"Shh," said Asher. "Most people would die for such a fancy setup."

The security guard studied his laced-up military boots as Soni walked Asher out of the gate, glanced nimbly at the car as the male specimen drove away, and again tilted his head, avoiding eye contact with Soni as she strode into the driveway. She knew the staff gossiped feverishly: that she, an unmarried Muslim woman, had taken to inviting a middle-aged man into her bedroom while her father was away on business.

She jogged back to her room, withdrew a Xanax from her drawer, and slipped it into her mouth.

⌒

WHEN SONI BEGAN SLEEPING with Asher, her mind contemplated, for long moments, the miracle of physical contact: grazing the sweatered edge of Asher's arm, his leg, the jut of his shoulder to affirm, in the incidental light of day—as she skipped down the stairs of his gym, he at her side—the tenderness she felt for him.

He was forty-seven years old, yet his body bore none of the unkind smears of age. He had sturdy, muscular legs; a pert, smooth ass; the ridged torso of an athlete: he'd been a professional squash player, Pakistan's most famous, only ten years before. Now he ran a gym in the basement of a coffee shop.

These days Asher's beaming face could be seen sliding up a screen—a box of detergent between his hands—on a digital billboard that swerved above an overpass in Lahore.

Soni had decided Asher's looks hewed to the old book of handsomeness: square jawline, brown eyes under a fringe of black lash, a nose that would've loomed large on a less arresting bone structure. The gray in Asher's hair became a mischievous afterthought, like a snaggletooth on a beautiful woman: the succumbing, teasing quirk of a faultless mold.

Asher worked out regularly, but like all his physical attributes that Soni had obsessively cataloged, his body had been granted the relief of beauty. The less he looked after himself—once devouring kababs and toast early in the morning, after Soni and Asher had had each other four times during the night—the better he looked. Asher rarely drew attention to his appearance. It was a habit born not of feigned modesty, Soni knew.

A timidity edged his grace.

One of the first things he said to Soni was "My father he studied—Lundun." His father had spent three months at a training workshop in Birmingham in the early seventies, but to Asher and his siblings, London constituted England.

And yet, Soni couldn't help but wonder, Asher hadn't been so timid when he'd walked up to her a month before while she jogged on the treadmill in his gym. "For few days now I've been seeing you're trying to trim your butt," he'd said, apropos of nothing. "But why? Your butt, it's not a Kardashian yoga ball. It's just a cute bubble. Let it be, kindly."

He'd said the words with soft, head-shaking dejection.

"That's *funny,*" Soni had blurted, her reaction tumbling with a kind of adolescent intensity designed to deflect.

Asher had pressed the up arrow on the left side of the machine. "Incline will improve heart rate. Good heart rate is must for stamina. Good stamina is must for daily happiness."

Soni had stared at her reflection in the glass wall in front of the line of treadmills, a thin smile pleated in the corner of her mouth.

Emboldened, she'd asked Asher if he was married, and he'd said, his lisp readying itself, that yes-th, he was married, and children were the *only* good outcome of marriage. Soni had remained silent, but Asher had smiled peacefully. "It's true, I promise-th."

~

FOUR DAYS AFTER they awoke in Soni's bedroom, Asher and Soni leapt out of bed, at dawn, in a hotel room. They brushed their teeth standing side by side at the sink. They rushed to Asher's car.

The November sun had scattered the color in Asher's eyes, flecks of brown strewn wheatgold. The silver hair at his temples, through which Soni's fingers had wandered all night in the hotel room, coiled in the gust of the car's heater. A strand curled boyishly over his eyebrow.

Beyond the car's windshield, as the sun rinsed the early-morning fog, birds bobbed on vacant roads. Lahore twinkled in a rare, emptied innocence.

Throughout the evening before, Asher had picked Soni up and plunked her, in shifting angles, on the square of the bed. "Are you enjoying?" he had asked, searching her eyes. "Are you enjoying, baby?"

Their bodies had surged together. Sex with Asher was liquid, hard, dissolving.

Asher's blue Corolla slowed at a traffic light and Soni reviewed the feuding urges of adulthood: the road to the left steered her to Cantonment, to home, to a life of loitering inside her cold old house; the right opened into Defence Housing Authority, a real estate scheme of seemingly boundless spread, in whose precincts Asher resided, and where Soni had arrived at parties in occasionally unlit streets, determined to drink from the fount of freedom.

Beyond the traffic lights a sweeper in yellow overalls crossed the road with a broom in his hand. His fingers were long, dry-knuckled.

"You see that man?" said Asher, pointing in front.

Soni nodded. "It's so cold."

"My being with you is like that man getting a visa to America."

Soni smiled politely.

She brought her hand over his. "I don't know if I'll be able to move today. I'm very sore from last night."

"Just leave it to me." He squeezed her hand.

Asher skipped down the stairs of the gym to open the doors—to the entrance, to the supply room, to the workout room—with different sets of keys, and Soni followed him silently, with solemn anticipation, like a child watching a grown-up access a storeroom of delights. He was wearing sweatpants, white Nikes, a blue sweatshirt with the hood over his head.

"By the way, have you ever done doggy style?" said Asher, as if asking whether she'd seen his misplaced shirt.

Soni shook her head.

"If you stick with me I guarantee you'll have fun." He switched on the lights. Energy-saver bulbs drooped from their sockets like gloomy hanging fruit.

"You know what a cow look like when she chews fodder?" He rotated his jaw in a square—left, down, right, up. "Most women look like this in bed. Not you. You're damn alive. Looking at you, hard to tell!"

Soni giggled.

Asher opened a cupboard and pulled out two green mats. He unrolled them in the center of the gray rubber flooring, and Soni sat cross-legged on one. The mats had withered, their foamy plumpness shrunk by overuse.

"A woman should be so strong that she's gentle," he whispered. "So graceful that she look like a queen in joggers-th."

He slid up on top of Soni and held her face in his hands. "Exactly like you."

The more he complimented her in his galloping way, the surer she was of his simplicity.

"The floor is hard," said Soni. "Let's go shopping for new mats."

"Allah will give."

The advertisement of Asher in a green shirt holding a box of detergent in his hands crackled on the flat screen mounted on the wall. Soni gripped Asher's wrists and smothered them with laughter. "Those khakis are *sooo* tight."

"Wore them only for you. So you could check out my butt. Swear on Allah."

He lay on her and breathed into her neck.

Soni lifted his shirt up and started peeling down his sweat-pants.

"First we exercise!" He held her hand and kissed it softly. "Twenty-five push-ups to warm up. See? You don't have to move your legs. Chin up, back straight. Inhale down, exhale UP. We have just thirty minutes before we open for business."

Despite his forty-seven years, Asher Naqvi professed scant interest in history, politics, books. He had no interest in the news because it was foul—like a peacock looking at its ugly feet, he explained. People have unique strengths, he advised Soni. Growing up a professional athlete meant having had to defer a life of intellectual pursuit. He could, however, teach Soni how to be street smart. In return, all he wanted was her affection. Soni would nod and smile, but she knew ignorance was a nicely plausible choice for good-looking, well-nourished people, like the celebrities whose lives she followed on social media.

Asher would frequently mention his children, laughing with full-throated rapture at the jokes of his ten-year-old. Soni had not met his son or daughter. She longed to see their faces in person, to discern Asher's lips and nose and quirks so she could relive him anew.

Later that morning, after Soni and Asher had held each other's slick bodies in the seclusion of his locked gym, they drove to her home.

An open sewer gushed beside the road winding out of the gym. It had rained, and the trees whistled, green-purple, beaded with water.

Asher's Corolla passed a moss-smothered roof, a dripping railed balcony. Mist rose from a manhole. Ferns sprang from seams in cracked walls. The air rang of monsoon rot, a sweet-sour fustiness so familiar to Soni, even in the winter.

Soni's father, a real estate tycoon, was in Islamabad for a meeting: they could snatch a few hours at her home.

Asher parked his car outside Soni's gate.

Her room contained a sofa, two chairs, and a low-lying white table placed at a distance from her bed. Above Soni's bed a mini black chandelier dangled from iron rods wrapped in jute rope.

Soni and Asher sat on her bed. "My feet are always cold," she sighed. "Like I'm fine otherwise but my feet are icicles."

Asher lifted her feet in his hands, as if examining a delicate tray. He proceeded to kiss them slowly, calling her his soul, his life. "You are my Princess Diana," he said with a sleepy smile. He pronounced it Day-yaana.

She ran her hand through his flopping, boyish hair.

"I've just realized," said Asher. "The way we have to hide to see each other. The big gates in your house. The security. The *tish-tosh*." He stroked her foot. "Your father is an important man. All my life my dream was to be with someone classy. Like you."

The statement should've caused Soni to recoil, she thought, to instantly mark the speaker as a buffoon.

She considered his words with the solemnity with which they'd been uttered. It was a folksy honesty she'd not encountered in her circle in Lahore.

"You're so much more famous than him," she said, thinking of the time she was in the living room while her father had watched a finals match in which Asher was playing. Fifteen years before.

"Fame can't buy class," said Asher. "Even I know that." And he chuckled sadly, comically, to himself, gazing at Soni's feet.

When Soni's father first began working at a small real estate business—from which he started his own company, Eagle Enclaves—he'd arrived at work on a bicycle. Now he traveled to his three-storied office in a bulletproof Land Cruiser. Like those of most rich people, his current life seemed marked by a mild obsessiveness that flowed from having and managing too much money: he exuded the flattened paranoia of a multimillionaire.

The year before, Soni's mother had died of ovarian cancer. Soni's father had provided his wife with lavish care in London, but a few weeks after her death he began a very public affair with his secretary, Huma, showing up with her at the inauguration of one of his housing schemes and requesting, with a show of his Rolex-heavy hand, that Huma cut the ribbon. The photo had appeared in the city pages of the newspaper the next day.

It had occurred to Soni the affair had probably started while her mother was still alive.

"Sonu!" said Asher. "Where is the princess lost? Thinking

all the time!" He grabbed Soni's legs and entangled them in the warmth of his.

"I was thinking of my mother," said Soni, smacking a pillow behind her.

Asher sat up and embraced her. He told her they were two peas in a pod. He'd lost his mother just after he'd won his first—and only—international trophy, the British Open Squash Championship, at the age of thirty-five. Did Soni know it was one of the two most prestigious international tournaments in squash? Well, he had not returned to the game. Walking away from his seat of glory had been difficult. No matter that he was thirty-five and unlikely to sustain a winning streak. Give the world a winner, he said in Urdu, and they'll obliterate you with their love. The Pakistani Ministry of Sports had urged him to continue playing. He was tired, he said; his knees throbbed. The knowledge of how much one's body could endure was a truth only a player—not even his coach—glimpsed. Once he'd decided to retire, he felt calmer, lighter. The endorsements continued to pour in. He bought a small house and asked his father to live with him. "We're not millionaires like you," he said. "But we're happy in our humility."

"Like him, you mean," said Soni. "I'm not a millionaire."

"But you will be." Asher smiled. "It's only a matter of time."

Before Asher parachuted into her life, Soni would spend most weeknights out, eating with friends, desperate to subject her heart to moments of connection: she was not alone in the world. There existed people who cared, who texted her gossip from their lives. People are nice to girls who don't have mothers, thought Soni.

It was after her mother's passing that Soni had turned to Xanax. Her mother's death had carved her up and put her back somewhat differently. It started simply: a Xanax when she couldn't sleep, once a week. When she found herself reaching for the hard silver strip every day, she knew she had a problem.

With Xanax in her veins, the pain began at last to slip past her, and Soni found happiness that folded itself—effacing, fetal—to live alongside her desolation.

Hair wet from the shower, high heels on her feet, Soni would reach for a Xanax before leaving for a party. It was as if she were starting anew, unsoiled by the catastrophes of her world.

Lying slovenly in her bed, twisting a strand of hair around her finger, Soni could hear, outside, the shuffling click of boots on brick: a security guard was doing a round in the early afternoon.

Her phone buzzed. She tapped the video request.

*"Jumma Mubarak,"* smiled Asher. He brought his lips to the screen and kissed it. "No harm in remembering Allah sometimes."

"He's always in my heart . . ."

"Tell me about your fantasies."

"What fantasies?" asked Soni.

"Didn't you fantasize about me before we made love?"

"Fucked, you mean."

*"Taubah!"*

"I want to hear yours." Soni smiled provocatively, leaning into the phone.

"I imagined you coming to my house," said Asher. "My poor little house. And I imagined you liking all the rooms!"

"Oh."

"I imagined you meeting Abba in his room upstairs. I wish you could meet him. He would love you."

"Your most burning fantasy . . ."

"I love you for knowing that."

"You're lucky to have a good relationship with him."

"When Abba gets even a little unwell, I panic. He's everything to me."

"You're a good son."

"I'm sure your father loves you very much," said Asher. "His only child. His blood. His life."

"And then what did you imagine?" she asked, hurriedly, before Asher began telling her, as he had once before, oblivious of her anger at her father, that she ought to respect him.

"Shit, I got to go," said Asher. "Love you, bye."

This was how it was with Asher.

She rolled over and pressed her face into her pillow.

The next night, when Soni called Asher, the phone rang and rang. At 2:00 a.m., he rejected her call with an accompanying text: "T in my room tonite. Sorry babe." T was short for Tanya, and Soni had begun calling her the same to exile from her mind the real identity of a real wife.

The following morning, Soni indicated her annoyance: Asher had disappeared again; she wished he had conveyed he'd be unavailable.

"I'm so sorry," he gasped, looking at the screen of the phone. "It was totally sudden. She came and sat in my room. That's what wives do. They come, they sit."

"And then what happened?"

"And then she was just there."

"Doing what?"

"Sorting out her clothes in the cupboard."

"And?"

*"Buss."*

*"Buss* what?"

"I hated it," he said.

"Hated what?" A nauseous sensation, distinct from her anxiety, crested in Soni's stomach.

She said, "Then why did you do it?"

"If I don't it will look suspicious."

"How much do you do it?"

"I try to avoid as much as possible."

"How often?"

"Maybe once in six months."

"How does it happen?"

"Sonu, please."

"I want to know."

"You don't want to know."

"I *want* to know."

"You'll get angry."

"I promise I won't."

"Yes you will. Just leave it. It means nothing at all."

"But I really want to know."

"Don't you know men? We can just do it."

"How, if you don't want to?"

"Men are dogs-th."

"How!"

"You'll get upset."

"Just *tell me.*"

"Do you know anything about cricket?"

"I live in this country for God's sake."

"So imagine the Pakistan cricket team is playing in Perth. It has rained. The wicket is wet. The eleventh batsman, who is basically not a batsman but a bowler, is standing at the wicket. He has no choice but to bat. And the bowler is Brett Lee. What will the batsman do? *Eyes closed, bat forward.* That's what it's like doing it with your wife."

"That's so sick."

He was quiet.

He said, "You're feeling humiliated."

"Excuse me?"

"You feel humiliated. Am I right?"

She wondered how the thoughts in his head, forged in Urdu, were released so quickly and bizarrely into the English wild. She told him she wanted to sleep because, as the mental doctor had correctly diagnosed, she felt "humiliated." Asher apologized. He promised it would not happen again. As he brought the phone closer to his face to say goodbye, it slipped out of his hands onto the bedsheet. When he picked it up the passing glimpse of a small face, shut asleep, blurred onto the screen. The video was quickly switched off.

What was Asher doing talking about sex as his child slept beside him?

There was the guilt, sparked by children she couldn't bring herself to adore—little humans who took up the place of pure, uncomplicated love in his heart. If Asher didn't love T, had never loved her—his words—how could he love the faces that bore her impression? And how could Soni feel piercing sympathy for his kids one moment, but find herself unable to celebrate their existence? She was losing her mind. The next day Soni resolved not to take Asher's calls.

He called her twelve times. "How busy are you that you can't talk to me???" he texted. When Soni eventually called him back, at 2:00 a.m., he picked up the phone and pleaded: "Don't ever ignore me like this. If my kid is sleeping next to me, I will go to the bathroom to tell you I can't talk. Just don't ignore me, please."

Soni thought of her impasse: she didn't have anyone in her life to whom she could turn. She had told her best friend, Sarah, about Asher, and Sarah had been more brutal than Soni had anticipated: you're going to be called a home-wrecker, Sarah had said. "A man can do whatever the fuck he likes," she'd texted Soni. "Men get to boast about relationships such as this. PS: Can't believe you shacked up with HIM! Not exactly an Ivy League type." Soni had reeled, changed his name on her phone, and pledged not to tell anyone. On the phone Asher assured Soni that his relationship with his wife had eroded a decade before he'd met Soni: he'd had three affairs before she came along, he said tenderly. Soni had noticed the shift in mood, a fluttering feminine curiosity, when Asher walked into a public space. She'd experienced, too, the ease with which he'd approached her, engulfing her in his unlicensed world.

Asher spent an hour whispering sweet nullities into the phone. Soni listened silently. "If I agreed to marry you, would you cheat on me, too?" she finally asked. He told her he did not wish to be murdered by her father. Soni clasped the phone hot against her ear, but her thoughts drifted to the thrum of panic. She thought of a simpler time, when her mind was unmapped by the terror of sleeping with a married man. She felt wretched for marring his already broken family.

"Please don't be offended," Asher said, noticing Soni's silence.

"But it's not you who's made my marriage bad. I realized two days after I married T that it was a mistake."

"Why did you marry her?"

"Pressure. My family."

"You were an adult."

"Not everyone is as smart as Day-yaana."

"Answer my question."

"I didn't know what I wanted. And you were thirteen years old."

Three days later Asher was back in Soni's bed, stroking her hair. In the lamplight, closer to Asher's inner thigh, his skin shaded darker.

Soni grazed her finger along his pubic hair. "Under your armpits and even on your chest makes sense, but I don't understand why you have to spray Axe on your *balls*."

Asher tucked a strand of her hair behind her ear. "Cleanliness is a statue in Islam."

"Perfumed balls on the other hand . . ."

He drummed his fingers on his chest and cast his eyes farther down his torso. "Not bad, eh? Above average."

"I don't care about size."

"*Acha?* All women care. Just by looking at a man's face I can tell you how big he is."

"Is that what's on your mind when you talk to a man?"

"Unlike you, I don't talk to random men. Men you meet at the gym." He pulled Soni closer to him and said, "You're not going to believe but you're the first woman I've loved."

"Oh please!"

His phone rang.

"Can you put T on speakerphone?"

"Why?"

"I want to hear her voice."

Until now Soni hadn't had the courage to admit her fascination with Tanya.

"Anything for you," Asher said, and pressed the speakerphone button.

*"Assalamalaikum."*

The voice was richly feminine.

"What," he said. The word was uncorked from the gut: sharp, terminating.

"Where are you?"

"Out."

"When will you be home?"

"Soon."

*"Kab?"*

"Soon."

"Any rough idea when?"

"I said—soon."

"See you then," said T, the words dipped in a tentative glow.

When the phone beeped, Soni looked at him in disbelief. "What was that?"

"What?"

"Why were you rude to her?"

"I was not rude."

"You'd never speak to me like that."

"That's because I love you."

"You can try to be nice to her."

"Why are you taking her side?"

"She doesn't deserve to be 'humiliated,'" said Soni, feeling her own bizarre wellspring of sympathy as the words flew from her mouth. It was one thing to cheat on one's wife, quite another to be so churlish.

"I know you are Miss Know-It-All but you know nothing about being married," snapped Asher. "You should not give advice about T. I have to say 'soon' because I can't say I'll come home in the morning, can I? And when I go back I'll have to tell her that the party went on very late. That's my issue, my headache, my business-th. I'll handle it. It would be best if you didn't interfere."

Soni opened her mouth to speak. Then she saw herself as the lover declaiming from her perch about the woman she was helping him betray.

She knew she could never chide him on the matter. Unless she walked away.

"You're right," she said. "I should zip my stupid mouth." She kissed him on his nose. "Can I see her photo, please? Her Facebook page has tighter security than my house."

"Absolutely no. I don't come here to stare at my wife's photos."

The next afternoon when Soni returned from the gym, her father opened the front door.

"Home at long last!" he said, spreading his arms. He wore black jeans and a gray sweater. "Are you training for the Olympics?"

Soni ignored him.

"How come I never see you?" he asked.

"I didn't know you would suddenly be back from Islamabad today."

"I ask the staff where you are and I hear, 'Soni *baji* has gone out.' Out, out, out. Always out."

"What else should I do?"

"Design your jewelry. You're good at it. Why did you stop?"

"My mother died. You may or may not remember."

"Soni. Please. Let's not do this. Let's spend some time together."

"You have your own . . . life," said Soni. With her arm she wiped sweat off her forehead.

"If you wanted you could be part of that life."

"You have Huma. You're sorted."

"That same old childish shit."

"Good to know that's how my feelings are perceived."

"You've made no effort to get to know her."

"I have zero interest in getting to know your mistress."

"You should *not* speak about her like that. She's helped me through hard times."

"Please tell her to trim her toenails. Gives *a lot* away. Some friendly advice."

Soni walked past him, stopping, for a moment, on the first step of the stairs that led to her room, her hand clenched on the wooden ball at the base of the banister. Her heart flapped. If her relationship with her father continued in this fashion, she would lose not just the pieces of him from which she recoiled but the walking, talking fact of a father.

She looked back. He was gone.

She ran up the stairs in her sneakers and locked the door to her room. She remembered when her father had bought her sketchbooks to draw in. She had gotten into Royal Holloway in London, but her father had said no. Eighteen was too young an age to "send a daughter away." Soni's imbibing of Muslim norms and culture were of utmost importance.

She thought of the frantic sex she had with Asher in her bed, in her room, in her father's camera-rutted house. She felt good, wrought, sustained.

She thought of her father's unspoken but obvious plans for her: to marry well, to be a conduit to an even more sophisticated world.

She felt a mild savage pleasure now in her differences with Asher. She could marry Asher and her father would be rebuked.

Outside Soni's bedroom window the sky was a bruised metallic sheet. An *amaltas* smudged the horizon. Her hands slid open the bedside table drawer and she withdrew, without looking, a loose Xanax. She swallowed it with water.

She held up her hand against the lamplight, looking at her snaky veins, the riveted silver on a ring. She'd designed the ring the year before. She recalled the breathlessness with which people complimented her bracelets, ear cuffs, rings. At weddings, women came up to her to tell her how much they liked what she was wearing, and Soni had, three or four times, brainstormed with acquaintances on the kinds of designs they wished to have made. Her friends had urged her to start her own brand, but launching one required an end to late nights lying on her bed in temporary self-possession, an embrace of early mornings and the small, shattering surrender they drew from one.

Committing herself to a collection would be a way to burst forth from the shadows of her life, she thought. It would release Asher from the strain of making her happy. Soni could identify the exact moment when her heart would begin to dip: every time Asher dropped her outside her gate. In the short walk between the gate and her bedroom, Soni would become twitchy, her identity a niggling blank made from Asher's absence.

The next week Soni bought a ticket to London. When her father presented her with an envelope stuffed with the faces of Jane Austen and Queen Elizabeth, Soni said she had enough money for her trip. He grumbled something about "the importance of backups," but she replied she was handily backed up from the money he transferred into her account every month as payment for being a phony employee in his organization.

Asher chortled at the impulsiveness of Soni's decision as he watched her pack her bags on video. She was the only person he knew who could travel all the way to London on a whim. But if Princess Day-yaana couldn't fly to London because she felt like it, he said, who could? Soni told him she'd be meeting PR firms to discuss the scope for "contemporary Pakistani jewelry abroad." Asher smiled. "Nothing wrong with saying you're going to London because you feel like going. If you can't enjoy your money in your lifetime, what's the point of having so much?"

Soni frowned.

"In all seriousness, I'm really happy you're doing this, Sonu." Her first order, he said, should be a ring for Soni Chaudhary commissioned by Asher Naqvi. She should use green zircons— he winked on the screen—in place of emeralds.

The flat on Edgware Road smelled of Soni's mother: of almond oil, duck-feather down comforters that Soni and her mother had bought at John Lewis, a sweet medicinal whiff in the corners of the rooms. Her mother, relieved to have been free of the hospital, had hummed vintage Bollywood songs, giggled with Soni at night sprawled on her daughter's lap. She'd heated left-over *soujak* from the restaurant Maroush down the road, folded omelets with a flick of her wrist. Soni did not stop her mother from making breakfast for her. She knew it was the delicate, brave, exquisitely alert love of a dying mother.

During one of those nights, as her mother lay on Soni's lap, Soni had asked her what it was about her father that had attracted her. "Oh, his generosity," she'd said with a whispering clarity that suggested the question had rung in her mind all her life. "I was dazzled by it. He was so different from my own family. We never had money. But your father would buy a *chhalli* for ten rupees and give the *chhalli-wallah* one hundred rupees as tip. He loved to give." She had paused, and looked up at Soni's face. "Money, I mean. He was always generous with money."

Soni returned from lunch on Bond Street and, without taking off her jacket, sitting on the rim of the sofa, her knees clapped together, opened up her laptop. Asher was waiting.

She told him that he should visit her; they'd be freer in London.

He shook his head.

She said she would split the cost of his ticket.

"Please don't embarrass me."

"I didn't mean it like that."

"Abba is not well," said Asher. He was looking at the surface of the table.

"What happened?"

"Water in his lungs again. And he has suddenly become so weak. He slipped in the bathroom today."

"That's terrible. I'm so sorry. How is he now?"

"T took him to hospital. He fractured his leg. Just pray for him."

"Is T close to him?"

"Very respectful. Treats him like her own father."

"That's nice," said Soni, expressing genuine admiration, a sentiment she did not wish to probe. She knew Asher had said the words objectively, his praise for his wife distinct from his lack of feeling.

"Her brought-up was traditional," he said.

"And how is T doing?"

"Madam is becoming an Islamic scholar. She's going to Quran class every day."

"*MashaAllah,*" said Soni. She added: "I'm glad she's looking after your father."

Soni had daydreamed about looking after Asher's father. She would sit by his bedside, talk to him, arrange nutritious food for him. She knew she would do it with devotion.

As she opened her mouth to tell him this, Asher said he must go: his father needed him.

Soni was newly startled, every time, by how her English acquaintances exuded warmth iced with formality, even when they were happy. These were good people who worked hard, stuck to plans, who spoke gently of life. While she was with them, she said *thank you* relentlessly. Soni wondered how out of place Asher would be. He would smile, revealing his beautiful teeth, his belly-strong laugh. He'd laugh too much, in the way of handsome men, to compensate for conversation he couldn't offer.

While Soni met lank-haired publicists in toasty offices in Central London, Asher met with new clients at the gym. One evening, Asher posted a video on his Facebook page of a lion protecting a baby deer. He shared a sepia photo of his father as a young man, leaning against the hood of his car.

Soni had scoured Asher's Facebook page and found not a single photo of T. She imagined T looking after her father-in-law, her actions buoyed by the old and fixed notion of respecting an elder: no matter one's mood, a father-in-law needed to be fussed over. She imagined Asher's father defending T, berating his son for not appreciating his wife as he should.

When Soni returned to Lahore, ten days later, Asher came to pick her up from the airport. Sitting in the driver's seat in his blue Corolla, he looked like a model from a bygone era: he wore a sleeveless black woolen waistcoat buttoned over a white dress shirt; a maroon scarf was knotted around his neck. His wet hair fell into a wide parting. For a moment he looked like a boy with salt-and-pepper hair. He leaned over and kissed Soni on the cheek. "Thank God you're back. Just go *mad* without you here."

"Really missed you," Soni said. She cranked down the window: in came the peppery air of a choked city. She pinched her nose, willing away the brassy taste of fume in her mouth. Asher reached over and rolled up her window.

The cold had sharpened. In the late afternoon the sky was streaked with jets of white. Squat manicured hedges rushed along belts of newly paved airport road.

"Did you have fun with the Britishers?" he asked.

She told him she had, as a matter of fact, had fun. She had

bought him a cologne, a jacket, chocolates he could give to his kids.

"I'll wear the cologne only around you," he said. "So it can become my smell for you."

"That's exactly what I expected you to say."

He clasped her hand. "I know you think we are just having fun. But this is true love."

It was the kind of statement she'd gotten used to hearing from Asher: it made her heart prance.

They drove to a new hotel located in the far reaches of Lahore. As the Corolla passed a tree-lined boulevard, a redbrick art gallery, hotels clogged with queues of cars at security check-points, Lahore began to alter. Construction sites loomed in the dust. Rectangular grids, slick with grime, simmered in the sun. A crane was hoisting sacks and chains and beams from a dug-up crater, and the sun cleaved to steel like breath to a fogged windowpane.

The Corolla slowed at a traffic light. Soni looked at the small watchtower in the distance: a jutting gun, unmanned, faced the road. Perhaps the guard had fallen asleep, slumped on one of the sandbags inside his mini tower.

The hotel room was small, seedy, neat. A worn red carpet wound across the room. An apple and a congealing banana lay on a white plate suffocated with cling film.

Soni and Asher hugged each other silently, in a body lock, their hands around each other's sides.

"Just keep hugging," he whispered. "You bring so much peace in my life. Before I met you, I swear I didn't know I could be so happy."

"And you're my Xanax."

"*Nothing* can replace your Xanax."

She laughed, he kissed her laugh.

Soni climbed onto the bed.

Asher shuffled his knees onto the bed and held her face between his hands. He looked at her as if for the first time, his gaze steady. He kissed her softly. And the relationship slid from the transparency of lust to an admission of tenderness.

Soni exhaled with a sense of wonder that was also its own bewilderment. She had rarely experienced affection such as this.

Several hours later Asher took Soni to the bathroom, where he buttoned her shirt and fixed her hair with a white plastic hotel comb.

"Oh shit," said Soni, squinting in the mirror. "You gave me a hickey."

"Are you serious?"

"You were literally sucking on my neck a minute ago . . ."

"Look like a rash," said Asher, stroking the bite.

"I have concealer, but we have to stop being so reckless, dude." She jumbled through her handbag.

"So sorry."

She rubbed the makeup on her neck, sprayed Axe body spray over her shirt. She put on a sweater and glared at her reflection in the mirror.

Soni exited the room first, passing a dome camera in the hallway, a cleaning lady vacuuming the carpet. She smiled brightly. She walked with a calm, almost bored, gait to the elevator.

Ten minutes later Asher stepped out and walked, with a cool, forgetful air, to the same elevator.

They got into Asher's Corolla, and Soni wrung her hands. "I don't think anyone saw."

"Not a soul. Not a soul."

They drove around a roundabout patched with tufts of dry grass. Inflated swimming pools in sharp blues rested against a concrete wall.

When they arrived at Soni's house, Asher parked the car outside the gate.

"Don't fight with your father," he said. "Ignore if you have to. Just smile. It's *sunnah*."

Soni was looking at Asher when his mouth began moving in a prayer. "Shh." He continued to mutter and when he finally blew on her, he said, "Three prayers: one to keep away depression, one to keep away the evil eye, and one for safety. Now my love can go."

~

THE DAYS BECAME SHORTER. A bone-stiffing chill seeped into the early morning. For several days Soni woke to the sound of a bird drilling on the tree outside her window to fish for insects sleeping away the winter.

In the afternoon Soni's father left for Islamabad, where he would inaugurate a new housing complex. From her window Soni saw Huma sliding into the car with him, waving a gaunt finger at the housekeeper, reminding him to "look after" the house. Huma's lips were overdrawn with maroon pencil and her face had an air of clammed-up pride, as if she hadn't yet decided how to react, publicly, to her magnificent good fortune. Until two years before, Huma had filed papers and made phone calls and arranged meetings for Soni's father. In the evening, the company car had dropped her at her own home. Now, Huma lived in Soni's house, sleeping on the same left side of the bed where Soni's mother had rested her inky black hair for twenty-eight years of her marriage.

Asher arrived at Soni's house just after her father had departed.

He stripped to his underwear and got under the sheets in her bed. "Why don't you ever talk about marriage?" he asked, looking at her jute chandelier. "I want you to be my Mrs."

"We've been over this *many times*. You have a family already," said Soni, sliding in, clothed and socked and sweatered, next to him.

"They can be your family."

"Let's not go there, Asher."

"I will go when you come. I can bet on it."

"And your children?"

"Those two come with the package. The five of us will live in a small rented house together. I just want you and, trust me, everything will be fine."

*"Five?"*

"I can't leave Abba, can I?"

"I miss Mama so much," said Soni.

"My love." He stroked her cheek.

"Why do men stay with women they don't love?"

Asher was quiet.

"It's so cruel. Why didn't you leave her if you knew after two days of your marriage you'd made a mistake?"

"I tried."

"How?"

"I didn't have my first child for five years."

"That's ridiculous. You basically waited five years to be tied down." She got up from the bed.

"Now I have a beautiful son, so what's your point?"

"This is not about your son," she said, pacing her room.

"Why are you rubbing it in?"

"Why did you have a child with someone you didn't love?"

"My mother-in-law said having a child would fill the house with love."

"And when it didn't, you went and had another one?"

"How can you speak about my children like that?"

"I think we should take some time off," she said abruptly.

"Time off?"

"Not talk for two weeks. So we can think about our relationship. This is so unhealthy." She sat down on the bed.

"Think about what?"

"About how we want to proceed."

"This is not America that we take Time Off, Time Out, Time Up."

"I think—"

"First to get time off"—he smiled—"you need to put time *in*." He pulled Soni to his chest, under the grip of his forearm, and began tapping his fingers on the inseam of her jeans. "Time in," he grinned. "Before you can have time out."

"Do you know Diana was the ancient Greek goddess of *hunting*?" said Soni, desperate to change the subject.

"I thought it means Beauty."

"Uh. No."

"But the Princess was being hunted," said Asher. "Am I right? Am I right?"

"Someone's been spending time on Google, I see."

"Only to impress you."

"We're both *insane*," she sighed, tracing her finger around the edge of his red nylon underwear. She remembered her horror at glimpsing the nylon the first time he'd undressed in front of her.

"Did you call yourself a sex addict the other day?" she asked in a low voice. "A bit dramatic. But if you want to call yourself that, sex addicts should wear organic cotton. Nylon—big no."

"As you say." He laughed shyly and leaned in to graze his forehead against hers.

⁓

FROM THE OUTSET Soni had insisted they mustn't meet every day: she felt frightened when he left his family, often in the evening, to spend time with her. There was the shame of tearing Asher away from his son and daughter, who had no hand in their father's indifference to their mother, but it was also his blue Corolla parked habitually outside her gate.

On the days they didn't meet, Asher promised to call Soni just after midnight.

Soni would wait for his call: midnight turned to 1:00; 1:00 to 2:00; 2:00 to 3:00 a.m. She would imagine him sitting next to T, waiting for her to leave. She would imagine T sitting on the sofa and eventually moving to the bed, arranging a blanket over her delicate feet. Soni had pleaded with Asher, once, to say *one nice thing* about T. He'd said he supposed she had nice feet.

Lying on her bed, Soni thought of the incivilities that now infused their relationship. Her courtesy of speech had begun to coarsen. When she scolded him for being late to a date, he stayed quiet. When she shouted at him for not calling her back even though he said he was "just" calling her, he remained silent. When she shrieked that he should *say something,* open his mouth, he would say, "I get overwhelmed."

"Overwhelmed by what?" Soni would ask.

"When you scream, my mind shuts down."

"It makes things worse when you stay silent."

"You're the one who becomes unhappy. I'm so happy to be with you."

"Because you get to escape that life of yours, a life you have no interest in. I'm dealing with so much shame. On top of that your absentmindedness, and your stupidities, all the bloody time."

"Sorry I'm so stupid. You never used to call me stupid before."

"You've driven me to this point. And you can't even see it."

Once, Soni's anxiety had raced like skidding black clouds into the stretch of her mind. It had blanketed her in a pall. She took long, mindful breaths to calm herself. The first time she experienced an attack, she knew it was a sign of an incipient unhappiness. She texted Sarah to say she'd resolved to end her relationship with Asher.

"Good!!" Sarah's message sprang back. "Have been worried about you. End it NOW."

Soni called Asher to tell him she no longer wanted to be with him. "There. Is. No light. At the end of this tunnel." She squeezed the words out between breaths. Their situation was irredeemable: they'd have to cut things off without a tortured conversation about the perils of breaking up.

Her decision was sudden, elemental, purifying.

At first she didn't realize Asher's gasps were him sobbing on the phone.

"Are you leaving me?" he cried. "Please tell me you're not doing this to me. Are you *leaving* me?"

"I'm a mess. My health is a mess. This will never work out anyway. I don't want to do this anymore."

"Please don't leave me. Please, please *don't leave me*."

"This is not easy; don't make it harder for me, Asher. My anxiety is getting worse. I can barely function."

"I can't survive a single day without you. I'm totally lost without you. *Please* don't leave me. I feel like suiciding."

"Asher—"

He was weeping.

He sobbed quietly.

"Why should I not leave you?"

"Because you love me. And you are trying to *run away*. Don't do this. Don't run away from me like you've run away from everyone else. I will make everything good again. I promise. I will make you happy. Just don't go."

"Please don't cry like this. I don't want to see you cry."

He began weeping harder, the relief of Soni's overture, the prospect of her empathy, causing him to break down entirely.

Soni thought back to the early days of her affair, when she and Asher had been, in their private glee, showy and delighted.

Now a fear lurked at the edge of her throat.

When she told Asher of her unease, he said, between sniffles, that it would be wise to tell his friend Salman. Salman could cover up for Asher if T called him inquiring as to Asher's whereabouts. He gave Soni Salman's number, and told her to call him in the event of an emergency.

A few hours later Asher persuaded Soni to go on a drive with him. Lahore's roads were flooded with rainwater the color of milky tea; branches and rocks and plastic bags whirled in the stream.

In the rain they drove to a café in Defence Housing Authority.

As they waited for smoothies by a lime-green counter, loitering at a thoughtful distance from each other, an elderly lady walked up to Asher.

"Asher Naqvi?"

He smiled.

"Proud son of Pakistan. My son got into squash just because of you." She retrieved her phone from her purse.

"Can you please take the photo?" she asked Soni.

Soni nodded.

Asher locked his fingers in front of his waist. The lady smiled, clutching her purse in her armpit. Soni tapped the camera.

"Your daughter?" asked the woman.

"A very dear friend."

"Allah bless you both."

Soni folded her lips into a smile.

The waiter slid the smoothies to Asher, and Asher paid with his card.

"*That* was weird," said Soni five minutes later, shutting the door of Asher's Corolla.

Asher leaned over to take a sip from Soni's ginger-apple smoothie. "It's in our destiny to get married. I know you don't believe in fate. But one day, I know I will marry you. I just know it."

"Drop me home, please."

"I will leave if I announce our relationship to her. I can bet on it. I just want to tell the world. I damn care about the world."

"*Acha.*"

When Soni got home, she turned to her phone. "I was so embarrassed today. Our relationship is a joke. It's pathetic and we should *end* it."

The phone indicated Asher was typing. Twenty minutes later, a message swamped the screen.

*Seeing you is lifesaving medicine. It's like the medicine which Abba keeps under his tongue when he is suffering pain, and the moment he does this, everything gets under control. Please keep giving me the medicine of your face on a regular basis. I have parked on the road to write this, btw. You are very beautiful (with the perfect bubble butt) but I also love you for your sensitivity. You feel and notice everything. The way you speak about your mother in the softest manner. This is a beautiful sight to witness. When you talk, words flow like a river, sometimes very strong and sometimes very gentle. Your beauty is the mixture of spice and elegance. The spice of East and elegance of West. I am a Suzuki spare part and you are a Mercedes, but I have fit into the Mercedes somehow. My love for you is forever, so please don't leave me when you are feeling down. When you express doubt in this relationship, I all of a sudden cannot function.*

Her impatience at herself, for desiring him, was crippled by the knowledge that he nourished her in a primal way. His authenticity comforted her, but it also challenged her worst tendencies: casting an ungenerous eye to the way in which people spoke, their choice of clothes, the way they ate their food. When she was with Asher, one part of her observed his failings, while the other swayed, shrouded from the world, with the novelty.

Soni tapped open Facebook and typed in his wife's name. She'd toured from the margins of T's profile page before, but, every time, T's privacy settings had barred her. Soni returned again and again in a mania that lit her thirst: a photo, a video, a comment—anything would do. She now found herself hovering on T's page every day, tapping, hoping for a miracle.

The thumbnail showed, as it had done for weeks, a woman in a park, her back to the camera, her long brown hair wind-tossed. Soni tapped her finger on the photo for what must have been the fiftieth time.

The image enlarged.

She couldn't believe it.

She swiped to the left.

A fair forehead. Her nose a small, milky slope. Eyes glistening as they tipped, almond-like, at the edges. There were the full lips spanning a smile that bounced in the eyes. T was the essence of the kind of woman every Pakistani man dreamed to marry: fair, petite, exceedingly pretty. How could Asher have lost interest in her, and even if he had, surely her beauty, so total in its claim, made him, at his weakest, turn to her? Her breasts were not big. They were not small. They were certainly not smaller than Soni's. Where were the feet that had, two decades ago, moved Asher's soul? She clicked on an album titled "family!!" She zoomed in to one of the photos: it was grainy. She could see T grinning in every photo, clutching her children, her hands wrapped around them with youthful exhilaration distinct from the maternal ennui Soni had imagined. His daughter's eyebrows swerved fiercely upward, like her mother's. Asher had always told Soni that T was dull, shy, lacking confidence. In the photos, T herself looked like a child who hid her deepest sorrows everywhere.

The phone was ringing.

"My love!"

"Hi."

"What's wrong?"

"Nothing at all."

"When Day-yaana says 'nothing at all' it means atomic bomb is about to drop."

"Where is T right now?"

"Why?"

"She's so pretty."

"Huh?"

"How can you not be attracted to her? She's *so* pretty."

"Are you okay, Soni?"

"You have a very beautiful wife."

"Where did you see her?"

"Facebook."

"Why?"

"She changed her privacy settings."

"And now you're feeling humiliated."

"I don't always feel humiliated, Asher. Sometimes, like right now, I just feel very sad."

"Why?"

"We shouldn't be doing this."

"Stop being childish."

"Very childish to want to break out of relationship with a married man. Childish to hurt another woman. Childish to meet in hotel rooms. I'm a child. But you know what? You're an idiot."

"How can you talk to me like this? I'm coming to you right now."

"Absolutely not."

"I can't let you be alone in this state of mind. Your mind goes crazy. That's the price of intelligence."

"I don't want to see you."

"You've insulted me already. You might as well insult me to my face."

"I don't want to see you."

"Please relax."

"I'm going to shut the phone now."

"Soni, you'll go into a black hole. Just stand outside your gate. We'll go for a drive."

"I have an early morning meeting with a jeweler. I need to sleep. Plus, it's raining."

"Bring an umbrella."

"I'm in my pajamas."

"Take a shawl."

She took a Xanax.

In the car, Soni was quiet. She understood, for the first time, her own pathetic ruse: rushing to thwart the relationship and gamely surrendering her demands the next moment. What good was it to step back and recognize the lunacy spilling from their interactions if she wouldn't do anything about it? She knew she scrutinized her own gestures, but she'd begun to gaze not with the kindness of real introspection, but with the punitive inquiry of the present: a woman trailed always by her own shrieking effigy of herself.

The Xanax not only had calmed her nerves but also would dull her reactions to Asher, which was what Soni wanted.

At 1:00 a.m. the streets around her house were deserted. She looked outside the car window: raindrops dropped and slipped on the glass. The sky rolled like wet concrete. The pavements bubbled.

"You're all of a sudden getting very angry these days," said Asher.

"I should hide how I'm feeling?"

"Please don't hide anything. But why suddenly so angry?"

"You keep bringing up marriage. How can I possibly marry you?"

"We love each other."

"You have two children and a wife you don't have the balls to divorce."

He looked at her. "Am I hearing right? Are you expressing interest in marriage? I'm surprised."

"A good emotion. Better than numb."

"You should know that T told me she's sick of me. Maybe that's why she's opened up her Facebook. A wife can tolerate her man looking here and there. But something serious? She can smell it. I haven't spoken to T properly in a whole month. You should see our house. It's like a graveyard."

Asher slowed the car under a tree and switched off the ignition. He placed his finger on the fogged glass and squeaked out a heart. "My heart used to be pretty small. God promise-th. It has grown big because of your love."

Soni narrowed her eyes. "Is that Huma's car?" She pointed to a black Audi turning into the street where they were parked.

"Yes. It's her number plate."

"Fuck," said Soni, and she ducked. "Reverse your car."

"Relax. In the rain they can't see anything."

She thrust her head up. "Who is 'they'?"

"There was a man sitting next to her."

"How the hell do you know her number plate?"

"I know the number plates of all your cars. By the way," he said, "do you know I just finished reading a book?"

She knew this was a softening non sequitur.

"Which one?"

She wondered what Huma was doing out so late, on the roads.

*"Seven Habits of Highly Effective People."*

"And how did you like it?" She adjusted herself on the seat.

Who was the man sitting next to Huma?

"Concept was good."

"And?"

Should she tell her father?

"You should also read."

Soni turned her face away abruptly. "How will I ever accept your children?"

"They're part of the package."

"I know they're part of the bloody package."

"It's not nice being talked to like this by someone twenty years younger."

"I'm sorry. I just don't think I could ever love your children the way they *deserve* to be loved."

"You can do it. You're a fighter."

"A fighter addicted to pills."

"So what? Your life is not easy, but still you have the capacity to love. You're loving an idiot."

He took her hand in his and kissed it. Soni looked at his sinewy and chapped palms, the skin cracked, like stitches coming undone. She felt herself in the company of a man who rarely complained, his beauty more astonishing for the replenishments it neglected.

She placed her hand on his cheek. "Sorry about my moods. You're good to me. I should be the same."

"Please no sadness," said Asher. "When you're down everything becomes painful."

She nodded. The rain had stopped. The streets and trees and lampposts glistened in a weak orange glare.

"Please stay like this," said Asher. "Don't become angry with me tomorrow. Okay?"

"I promise."

"It's the most stressful thing in my life when you're upset with me."

"I promise."

~

DEEP WINTER GLIMMERED, then vanished, like a sunbeam. Soni's own comment, critical of herself for taking the Xanax, had tunneled into her mind. She promised herself she would go three days without Xanax. She downloaded a meditation app and, on the first night, fell asleep quickly to the sound of artificial rain. She slept and slept, her limbs slack with depletion. It was exhaustion, she knew, not of the body. Her mind was finally unclenching.

The next day, she grew unbearably restless.

She stayed up all night, drawing in a sketchbook, drinking chamomile tea, browsing the Internet. At 6:00 a.m., her mind yielded to the sudden weight of sleep.

A few hours later, she roused herself, took a shower, and drove to a jeweler's home, a labyrinthine interior in the old quarter of Lahore crammed between a fast-food joint and a shop that sold leather goods. Soni discussed with the jeweler a salary package as she dipped cumin-flavored biscuits in chai. She didn't have a plan: she was trying to convince herself of the possibility of one in the future.

On the drive back home, Soni stopped by a roadside florist

and bought two dozen roses. She arranged the flowers in her room and placed a vase in the drawing room.

A light rustled in Soni's mind. Perhaps they *were* meant to be together. She felt the tiny shards of anxiety—those that had clung to her bones, lingered in the flutter of her hands as she talked—drift into the air. Asher had, unbeknownst to him, demonstrated to her the meaning of kindness. His was a temperament that shielded itself from the affected sobriety of adulthood. He was sunny and jovial, every day, no matter the stirrings of his inner life. Deep down, or perhaps just below the hot surface of his skin, did he hate having to play the clown who made her smile by consuming his own sorrow, letting the ache crackle under his tongue?

She resolved to be kind to him.

When at night the blinding need for a Xanax tore into her, she rushed to the gym, often as late as 11:00 p.m. She ran on the treadmill. She ran and ran till the tendons in her thighs vibrated with pain.

For six days Soni awoke and slept without reaching for Xanax. Her mind stretched itself into an open white space like an empty auditorium in which the slightest sound echoed, affirming the stillness, the silence in which she rested. She was beginning to befriend herself.

In sharp clusters the February sun bounced off the windows in Soni's room. She looked outside. The air was clean, strung with light. A variety of plump pink rose flushed across the garden. After months of cold, of the smell of smoked wood lingering in hair and clothes and sofas, the air hummed with the first churning of spring—trees stranded tipsily in light, a scent of splashed brick and trimmed wet grass.

Her phone rang.

"I'm up, I'm up, I'm up!" she said.

"Abba died this morning."

She felt queasy. She told him how sorry she was.

She repeated she was sorry. Her eyes filled with tears. She asked how it had happened.

He had died in his sleep.

"I love you. I'm here for you."

Asher was quiet.

"May I come to the funeral?" she asked.

"No."

"No?"

"Tanya will be there."

"I'll blend in with your friends. Nobody will notice."

"Tanya will be there. I just told you."

"You always said you wanted to announce our relationship to the world."

"I used to joke around." A sharp breath dislodged from his throat. "Why are you bringing up a useless joke right now? There's no place for you in my life. Please grow up. Don't contact me again. This is bullshit. This is over. This is what I called to tell you."

The line went dead.

Soni walked to her bed. She sat down on it.

For several minutes Soni continued to sit. It occurred to her she could call Asher's friend Salman. She dialed his number.

"Can I speak to Asher?"

"Sorry, who is this?"

"It's Asher's friend Soni."

A pause. "I can ask him to call you back. Unless it's urgent. He's meeting some people right now."

"Where's Tanya?"

"He's, umm, he's hugging her."

She imagined his tears soaking her shirt. Wetting her neck. Trickling to her breasts.

Soni ended the call and fell slack on her bed. Behind her rib cage, the ricocheting of panic, circling the bones, pressing down. Her anxiety had always moved with an animal stealth. She squeezed her eyes and focused on her breath.

She gripped the ends of the bedsheet.

Needles on her arms. On the soles of her feet. Jabbing them.

Her toes twitched.

Her right leg tingled.

She squeezed her eyes and focused on her breath.

This was different.

And again, needles on her arms. On the tips of her fingers.

Just then, the maid knocked on Soni's door to bring in her morning tea. Soni quickly sat up on the edge of the bed, the bedsheet throttled in her fist.

Soni found herself speaking in a soft voice. She found herself thanking the maid repeatedly—for setting the tray on the table, for pouring the tea, and again, in a weak voice, for pouring the milk.

The words were an attempt at withdrawal from the self.

The maid looked at Soni with bottled-up puzzlement. She said nothing.

When she left, Soni drank down two Xanaxes with a sip of tea and collapsed onto the bed, curling her knees to her chest.

She awoke an hour later.

Soni's interactions with her father's staff—the only people with whom she came into contact during the day—became defined by a wan courtesy. She ignored how or in which way the security guards stared at her; she said *Assalamalaikum* with quiet determination. It was as if by her being kind to those around her, the sorrow within her confused itself, for a brief moment, to feel like a raw tenderness.

In her room Soni opened her laptop. Her fingers flew over the keyboard. Facebook, brutally obliging, spat out "Tanya Naqvi" as soon as Soni had typed in "T."

Tanya's profile photo had changed. The image was now of Asher's father, his beard white, his eyes soft with knowledge. Asher had the same sloping forehead, glint-brown and veined: veins through which, Soni couldn't help but think, blood had whipped to his dick in rapture at seeing her.

She scrolled to read Tanya's words about her father-in-law, a man who'd taught her, "Allah rewards those who are Patient with their Grief."

A moment later Soni was sitting in the back of her car as the driver moved the wheel with only the tip of his finger.

She would watch from outside Asher's house.

Would Asher personally escort his guests? Would husband and wife walk out together?

His house was fifteen minutes away.

She dialed his number.

She canceled the call.

Her heart hammered.

The car sped along.

To face the world was to face noise.

Her passivity was protective.

She became sealed to the clatter around her, guarding something within that, if touched, would spill out, revealing her brokenness.

"Where do you want to go, Soni *baji?*" the driver was asking.

"Umm, Hyperstar."

Moments later she walked into the fluorescent assault of a supermarket. Her mind zeroed in on the makeup aisle. She bought a lipstick. The cashier swiped the lipstick, pressed a key, and the notes, dusty under silver clasps, came spitting out in a black plastic tray. Soni focused on the rise and fall of her breath. She couldn't tell if she was breathing right. She knew the only cure for her pain was the experience of cradling it—its particular graininess, the sudden inner boil. She didn't have the strength.

She walked back to her car. Her legs were moving slowly. Her head whirled.

.

Back in her room Soni thought of calling Asher, of pleading with him the way he had with her. In the fragile latch of her mind a scene played again and again: Asher begging her not to leave, weeping.

She'd wondered when she'd grow tired of his loving banalities. She looked at her phone, at Asher's name saved under "Boy."

And she wept.

She wept in her bed, reacquainted with the violent intimacy of crying alone.

She wailed, cupping her hand to her mouth.

She trembled under the bedcover as her phlegm and tears streaked the sheets.

She clutched a pillow and cried. *He was done with the relationship.*

She wept in front of the bathroom sink, splashing her nose with water. To look at her own face, at the grisliness of her bloated eyes, was to acknowledge she was weeping for Asher. Her stomach, empty, pumped a fusty hot air. Her breath stank.

She dialed his number.

She aborted the call.

She texted him: "Is this really over?"

A day later, Huma knocked on Soni's door.

Soni got up from her bed, her phone in her hand. Asher had not responded.

"May I come in?" The voice was hesitant, a tone Soni did not associate with Huma and her lipstick-crusted mouth.

Soni opened the door and motioned for Huma to take a seat on the sofa.

"The maid says you're not eating," said Huma. "She says you have a bad cold."

Soni sat next to her. It was the first time in two days Soni had chosen to sit somewhere other than her bed.

Soni looked out the window, at the spirals of smoke rising above the neighbors' wall. "It's just a flu."

"Do you want some medicine?"

"I'm better now." She took a deep breath. "Thanks."

Soni got up to bolt the window. "Did my father send you here?"

"Your father hasn't been in the city for the last three days."

"Ah."

Huma got up from the sofa; she came and stood next to Soni. She said she was worried about Soni's health.

She asked if Soni wanted to see a doctor.

"Actually, there's something you can do for me," said Soni.

Huma looked at her uncertainly.

Soni told her she wanted to move out of the house.

Huma repeated Soni's statement to her.

"That's correct. This house. I'm starting my own business."

"I know you don't like me, but your father and I care about you."

Soni looked at her hands.

"Where will you go if you move out of the house?"

"An apartment."

"Okay. I'll talk to him."

Soni bit her lip; she nodded.

Huma walked to the door. "Your room will always be your room. I hope you know I won't let anyone use it."

Soni ignored the comment for its vacant theatricality. Her heart, filled with a vaster, lapping darkness, did not wish to court stupid nostalgias.

The door clicked shut as Soni looked out the window. Her eye trailed a wisp of smoke until it vanished into the air.

⁓

SONI SPRANG AWAKE at 6:00 a.m., her heart racing. For a moment she wasn't sure where she was.

She switched on the table lamp and a picture emerged: there were the chairs, and the table, and as she gazed up, her tiny black jute chandelier.

She fumbled for her phone. Asher had not replied. Her hand thrashed for Xanax in her bedside drawer.

She swallowed two pills without water and felt their bitterness explode on her tongue, on the roof of her mouth, inside her throat. She squeezed her eyes and swallowed her saliva. Her heart was still beating wildly.

She pulled on a pair of jeans and a sweater.

A leaky sun rose above Lahore's trees, stirring sunshine into the smog.

She reversed a red Honda Civic from the driveway.

A grimy breeze churned the air.

Soni neared the overpass that linked Cantonment to Defence Housing Authority and parked the car on the side of the road.

Asher's grinning face blinked on the billboard. She couldn't bear to look at it. She stared at it, tears gliding down her face.

She dialed Sarah's number.

"Everything okay?" Sarah's voice was rough, gnarled in sleep.

"He ended it."

"I thought you ended it ages ago."

"No."

"Where are you?"

"Out."

"Where?"

"On the road."

"Where exactly? Are you okay?"

"Under the Cantt overpass."

"Okay—I'm coming."

"Feel a little sick."

"Like how?"

"Like I'm going to throw up any second."

"Give me ten minutes."

"I want to see him, Sarah."

"Don't move. I'm literally brushing my teeth and coming."

"His father died."

"I don't care if his father died."

"How can you say that."

"Stay where you are. Don't move."

"I love him."

"Let me get off the phone, Soni."

"I want to see him."

"Don't move."

"Can't breathe."

Soni laid her head on the wheel; the phone toppled to the floor of the car. The sun glimmered on her forehead.

# Acknowledgments

Thank you, Franklin Foer, for your generosity many years ago when I was just starting out.

Fatima Burney was my earliest, most steadfast reader. I am so grateful for her time, her warmth, her interest.

Isaac Chotiner was an early champion of the stories. This note, which has been lightly edited for length and clarity, is just to say thank you—for a decade of friendship and solidarity.

I live between Lahore, Karachi, and San Francisco. My life in these cities is made possible by the love and affection of:

Adel Barrett, Adnan Malik, Adnan Siddiqui, Afia Aslam, Allie Wollner, Amina Mehdi, Arjumand Rahim, Fahad Hussain, Faiz Ghaffar, Fatima Salahuddin, Hamna Zubair, Jalal Salahuddin, Komail Aijazuddin, Khadija Rahman, Laila Ghaffar, Mehrunissa Khan, Mehreen Zahra-Malik, Moni Mohsin, Mubarik Imam, Naira Kalra, Natasha Telepneva, Radhika Jain, Rema Taseer, Saba Ahmed, Salman Toor, Sharmeen Obaid-Chinoy, Shazad Ghaffar, Sohail Salahuddin, Syed Zaheeruddin Ahmed, Tina Wahab, Wahab Mehdi, Zainab Mehdi.

I don't know what I would do without Hira Nabi and Zohra Rahman.

My thanks to my agent Melanie Jackson who took me on when I had very little to show by way of writing material. My conversations with you, dear Melanie, keep me going.

My thanks to Akhil Sharma, whose story "Cosmopolitan" inspired me to write "Mini Apple."

Sonny Mehta had faith in this book when I was just starting out, and I wish he'd been around to read it.

My editor Robin Desser pushed me to go deeper, to ask questions I was afraid to ask. I am forever grateful.

Faiza Khan knew and understood this thing before I knew and understood this thing. Thank you, dear Faiza.

Diana Miller swept in at a time of transition. Her kindness and her brilliant eye have made this a better book.

Ali Sethi, my ally in life and in all things creative, I love you.

My father—who was a bookseller before he was a journalist—has always encouraged me to write. His nonintrusive support is an enormous comfort in my life.

While I was in San Francisco, my mother took care of my dogs. I am deeply grateful. I have been informed that the dogs are now hers. Everything good and true in my life is because of her.

I am lucky to be married to the person with whom I have the most fun. Thank you, Bilal, for making a life with me on two continents. I am a better artist because of you.

### A NOTE ABOUT THE AUTHOR

MIRA SETHI is an actor and a writer. She grew up in Lahore and attended Wellesley College, after which she worked as a book editor at *The Wall Street Journal*. Sethi regularly appears in mainstream Pakistani drama series on television. She lives in Lahore, Karachi, and San Francisco.

A NOTE ON THE TYPE

This book was set in Granjon, a type named in compliment to Robert Granjon, a type cutter and printer active in Antwerp, Lyons, Rome, and Paris from 1523 to 1590.

Linotype Granjon was designed by George W. Jones, who based his drawings on a face used by Claude Garamond (ca. 1480–1561) in his beautiful French books. Granjon more closely resembles Garamond's own type than do any of the various modern faces that bear his name.

Composed by North Market Street Graphics,
Lancaster, Pennsylvania

Printed and bound by Berryville Graphics,
Berryville, Virginia

Designed by Cassandra J. Pappas